2/99

Mandie® Mysteries

MANDIE®

AND
THE LONG
GOOD-BYE

Lois Gladys Leppard

BETHANY HOUSE PUBLISHERS
MINNEAPOLIS, MINNESOTA 55438

Mandie and the Long Good-bye
Copyright © 1998
Lois Gladys Leppard

MANDIE® is a registered trademark of Lois Gladys
Leppard.

Cover illustration by Chris Dyrud
Cover design by Eric Walljasper

Published by Bethany House Publishers
A Ministry of Bethany Fellowship International
11400 Hampshire Avenue South
Minneapolis, Minnesota 55438
www.bethanyhouse.com

Printed in the United States of America by
Bethany Press International, Minneapolis, Minnesota
55438

ISBN 1–55661–557–4

To all the
MANDIE® FAN CLUB members

Because of all you thousands and thousands of members in over forty countries and every state in the Union, I am still writing Mandie Books, and as long as you read them, I will continue Mandie's story until she grows up, falls in love, and marries.

I read every letter you write to me, but I get so many it's impossible to reply. However, I do love you all and appreciate your loyalty, also all the notes, pictures, and doodads you send me. I treasure them all and keep them in a safe place where I can take them out and look at them.

In the next Mandie Book, Mandie will grow a little older and things will start moving faster in time in the coming five books.

If you are not a member, write to the

Mandie® Fan Club
Post Office Box 5945
Greenville, South Carolina 29606
U.S.A.

With love and thanks,

Lois Gladys Leppard

About the Author

LOIS GLADYS LEPPARD worked in Federal Intelligence for thirteen years in various countries around the world. She now makes her home in South Carolina.

The stories of her mother's childhood as an orphan in western North Carolina are the basis for many of the incidents incorporated in this series.

Contents

"Never promise more than you can perform."

—Publilius Syrus, First Century B.C.

Chapter 1 / Where Did It Go?

"Are you sure y'all can't stay until at least New Year's Eve?" Mandie asked Joe Woodard as they sat on the bottom step of the long staircase in the Shaws' house. "After all, this is only the day after Christmas, and I don't have to go back to school until the day after New Year's."

"Sure wish I could," Joe told her as he ran his long fingers through his tousled brown hair. "But my father has to go home to check on some of his patients, and he won't have time to come back just to get me."

"Doctors have an inconvenient life, don't they?" Mandie said with a smile. "And Dr. Woodard sure has his hands full covering all of Swain County and part of Macon County here."

"Oh, I suppose I forgot to mention there's a new doctor in Swain County now," Joe said. "My father said he's a young fellow just out of school but that he seems to be up on the latest medical knowledge.

9

His name is Oliver, Dr. William Oliver, and he's from some place in Virginia."

"Good, then maybe your father won't have to travel all over creation to see patients," Mandie replied.

"Oh, but this doctor has opened a regular office in Bryson City, so I suppose people will have to go into town to see him," Joe told her. "I don't believe he's planning on traveling around the country the way my father does. You know my father has always had an office in our house, but very few people have ever come to him. He goes to them."

"I'm glad you aren't planning to be a doctor," Mandie said with a smile, tossing her long blond hair behind her.

Joe quickly looked at her and asked with a smile, "Oh really? I wonder why?"

Mandie felt her face turn red, and she quickly stood up. "Just in case I decide to marry you when we grow up," she said. "I wouldn't want you running off for days at a time the way your father does."

Joe hastily rose and reached for her hand. "I aim to be a lawyer and to work in the town where we live," he told her. "No traveling."

Mandie pulled her hand away, and at that moment she heard someone on the stairs. She looked up the stairwell to see Jonathan Guyer hurrying down.

"I talked to my father," Jonathan began saying before he reached them. "And he says we have to leave on Monday to go home." He stepped down next to Mandie and Joe. "Since today is Thursday, that gives us three more days to do whatever."

"I have to leave today," Joe told him. "My father

has some patients to see, so I have to go with him and Mother."

"And we will be going home on Sunday," Sallie added as she came down the hallway toward the group. She joined them at the foot of the stairs.

Mandie laughed and said, "Then let's make hay while the sun shines. Time is a-fleeting."

"Just what do you suggest?" Jonathan asked.

"Well," Mandie said thoughtfully with puckered lips. "I suggest that we do whatever y'all suggest." She laughed again as she glanced around at her three friends.

Jonathan grinned, looked at Joe and Sallie, and, imitating Mandie's North Carolina accent, asked, "Well, now, what do we all suggest?"

"I believe it's almost noon, and I have to leave right after we eat," Joe said in a disappointed voice.

"Let's just go sit in the parlor until the food is ready," Mandie said, walking toward the front hallway.

Her friends followed and they found the parlor deserted. Evidently the grown-ups were doing something somewhere else. Snowball, Mandie's white cat, was asleep on the hearth by the fire, and he opened one blue eye to look at the intruders, then snoozed back off to sleep.

After they were all seated, Mandie said, "I'm so glad all of you came for Christmas. We've really had a nice holiday, and I want everybody to come back soon."

"Soon you must all come to visit the house of my grandfather," Sallie told them. "The Cherokee people would like for you to do that so they may become acquainted."

"I would very much like to visit your grandfather," Jonathan replied. "I have to keep reminding myself that you are Uncle Ned's granddaughter and that you live with him and your grandmother."

"Yes, my mother and father left this world before my memory," Sallie replied. She straightened her long, gathered skirt as Jonathan continued looking at her.

"Don't forget my house," Joe said, then turning to Jonathan he added, "And when you come to visit us, you can see Mandie's father's house where she lived before she came here to Franklin to live with her uncle John."

At that moment Polly Cornwallis, Mandie's next-door neighbor, appeared at the doorway to the parlor. "I just ran over for a few minutes to see what y'all are doing," Polly said as she came into the room and sat down next to Joe on the settee.

"We're waiting to eat, and then Joe will be going home," Mandie told her from where she sat in a chair nearby.

"Joe, you are going home!" Polly exclaimed. "But the holidays are not over yet." She pushed back her long, dark hair as she turned to gaze at Joe with her dark eyes.

"Oh, but I am the only one leaving today," Joe told her with a big grin. "Jonathan is not leaving until Monday and Sallie—"

"Jonathan, you will be here until Monday. Oh, how nice!" Polly interrupted Joe, quickly turning to Jonathan with a big smile.

Mandie smiled at Joe. She knew how Polly always followed Joe around whenever he came to visit the Shaws, and she realized that Joe was trying to get Polly's attention away from him and on to Jonathan.

Jonathan didn't seem interested in Polly. He shrugged and said, "Yes, I won't be going home until Monday."

"Home to New York!" Polly exclaimed, "Jonathan, you must give me your address. My mother and I will be going up there on our next holiday, which will be Easter, I believe."

"Oh sure," Jonathan said with a frown. "I'll write it down for you before I go home."

Mandie knew Polly had never been to New York, but she had. Mandie and her friend Celia Hamilton and Celia's mother had spent the Thanksgiving holidays at the Guyers' huge mansion in New York. And the three of them had solved a mystery after getting into a lot of trouble.

"Don't you forget now, you hear?" Polly was saying to Jonathan.

"Right," Jonathan said as he stood up and walked to the door. "M-m-m! I do believe I smell food!" he added.

Joe drew a deep breath and said, "I know I smell food."

At that moment Elizabeth Shaw, Mandie's mother, came to the doorway of the parlor and told the young people, "I'm afraid we have a problem with dinner, but it should be ready in just a little while. I'll let you know when." She turned to go back down the hallway.

Mandie quickly jumped up and hurried out into the corridor after her. "Mother," she called to her. Elizabeth stopped to look back, and Mandie caught up with her. "Will it be very long before we eat?" she asked. "Do we have time to do something else before it's ready?"

"No, I don't think so, dear," Elizabeth replied.

"The turkey just disappeared out of the oven—"

"Disappeared out of the oven?" Mandie interrupted, her blue eyes opened wide. "It disappeared out of the oven?"

Elizabeth smiled at her and said, "Yes, it just disappeared right out of the oven, but we do have ham already cooked from yesterday. So as soon as Aunt Lou can get that warmed up, we'll eat."

"Mother, you are saying the turkey just disappeared out of the oven? How did it do that?" Mandie asked, thinking she must have misunderstood.

"Aunt Lou was the only one in the kitchen. Jenny had run outside to her house for a minute, and Liza was upstairs. Jenny seemed to be gone too long, so Aunt Lou went after her, and when the two of them came back into the kitchen, the oven door was open and the turkey was gone," Elizabeth explained. "Now I do have to get back to our guests. They're all in the sunroom. Just be sure you and your friends don't run off somewhere." She continued down the hallway.

"But, Mother, weren't Mr. and Mrs. Burns supposed to be working here today, too?" Mandie called to her. The Burnses lived on the Shaw property.

Elizabeth slowed to look back and reply. "No, dear, they aren't coming to help until late this afternoon." She walked on.

Mandie quickly turned to hurry back to the parlor. This was a mystery! Who took the turkey out of the oven? And what did they do with it?

"Listen, everybody!" Mandie exclaimed as she entered the parlor where her friends were sitting. "Y'all won't believe this, but we have a mysterious theft." She sat down in a chair.

"What?" Joe asked, frowning.

"What did they steal?" Jonathan wanted to know.

"Do we have a mystery to solve?" Sallie inquired.

"My mother just told me that someone stole the turkey out of the oven, so dinner will be a little late," Mandie began.

"Someone stole our food?" Jonathan asked.

"Oh no, steal anything but the food," Joe said with a loud moan.

"Don't worry about dinner," Mandie explained. "We will be having the ham from yesterday, and I'm sure lots of other stuff. What I'd like to know is, who stole the turkey?" She explained to them what her mother had told her.

"And here I have to go home after dinner right in the middle of this mystery. How awful!" Joe said with exaggerated disappointment. "Y'all will never be able to solve this one without my help."

"I don't know about that. Remember, I'll still be here," Jonathan said to him.

"So will I," Sallie added. "What do we do first?"

Mandie thought for a moment and said, "We need to ask Aunt Lou some questions, but that will be impossible until after dinner. She'll be too busy. And then she has to have her dinner."

"Maybe we could just look for the turkey. I'm sure the very odor of it would help us locate it," Jonathan suggested.

"My mother told me we shouldn't go off anywhere before dinner," Mandie said, and then she added with a big grin, "But we could search the house."

"Now, why would anyone steal a turkey out of

the oven and then hide it somewhere in the house?" Joe asked. "I think that the turkey is long gone."

"Maybe they almost got caught and they just hid it somewhere and will get it out of the house later," Mandie said.

"But, Mandie, we would be able to smell it if it is in the house," Jonathan told her.

"Unless they put it in something that is tightly closed," Sallie suggested.

"You're right, Sallie, but what could something tightly closed be?" Mandie asked thoughtfully.

"Drawers, cabinets, bins—" began Jonathan.

Joe interrupted with a loud laugh. "Just don't forget one thing. That turkey would have been red hot if it was stolen out of the oven. So where would you hide a hot turkey?" he asked.

"On the other hand, it would have probably been too hot to carry off," Mandie said. "So what happened to it?"

"Do you know whether they just took the turkey itself, or did they take the pan with it?" Sallie asked.

"I don't know. Mother didn't say," Mandie replied. "I understand what you are thinking. If they took the pan, it would have been hot, and they would have had to leave the pan somewhere or put the pan and the turkey in something else. If they didn't take the pan, then they must have had something to put the turkey into."

"Yes," Sallie agreed.

"So how do you know whether we're looking for a turkey or a turkey with a pan?" Joe teased Mandie.

"We'll know that just as soon as I can ask Aunt Lou about it," Mandie told him. "I just can't imagine who would walk into the kitchen and steal a turkey right out of the oven.''

Polly had sat silently listening to the conversation. She finally spoke. ''You could all come over to my house for dinner. I'm sure our cook would have enough for everyone to eat.''

Mandie smiled at her and said, ''Thanks, Polly, but I don't think my mother would agree to that. You just stay and have dinner with us.''

Polly blew a deep breath and replied, ''I was hoping you'd ask me. You see, we still have those old cousins of my mother's at my house, and I just don't have anyone to talk to. Thanks, Mandie.''

''You're always welcome, Polly,'' Mandie told her. ''Now, if you're going to stay, you will have to help us find the turkey.''

''Of course, Mandie, but where do we plan on looking for it?'' Polly asked.

Mandie glanced at Joe with a big grin and, turning back to Polly, said, ''Who knows? We'll just have to look everywhere—the whole house, the attic, the cellar, and outside, too.'' Mandie knew Polly was afraid of the Shaw cellar because it was so dark down there.

''Well,'' Polly began slowly, then she looked at Jonathan and quickly said, ''If you're going with us, Jonathan, I'll help search.''

''Sure, I'm going,'' Jonathan said with a big grin. ''I'd like to find whoever stole that delicious turkey. I can just taste it. Mmm!''

''You aren't planning on eating it if you find it, are you?'' Polly asked with a look of concern on her face.

Everyone laughed.

Jonathan looked at Polly and asked, ''Now, why

else would I be chasing after a turkey if I can't eat it?''

"Well, I certainly wouldn't touch it. It may not be clean. Who knows where it's been or where it might be,'' Polly said, frowning and shaking her shoulders in disgust.

"But that's just what we are going to find out,'' Jonathan said with a nod.

"Whoever stole it might have eaten it up,'' Mandie suggested. "Why else would they take it?''

"They could be just playing a joke,'' Polly said.

"But stealing is not a joke,'' Sallie told her, then added with a smile, "especially when it's our dinner they stole.''

Snowball woke up, stretched, and came running to jump up in the chair with Mandie.

"Oh, Snowball, you must smell dinner,'' Mandie said, rubbing his head. Then suddenly looking at her friends, she added, "You know, Snowball could help us find the turkey. He would be able to smell it better than we could.''

"Oh, that white cat isn't that smart,'' Joe said.

"Oh, but he is,'' Jonathan argued. "Animals are smarter than human beings give them credit for.''

"But not that particular cat. I know him too well,'' Joe replied.

"According to what Mandie has told me about him, he has helped her solve some mysteries,'' Jonathan said.

"All he knows to do is run away,'' Joe said.

Mandie could see the two boys were becoming involved in an argument, even though they had finally become friendly toward each other after meeting at her house for Christmas. She had to stop them from getting into a strong disagreement.

"All right, Snowball is smart sometimes, and then sometimes he is not so smart, so let's just make our plans to look for the turkey," Mandie said emphatically as she straightened up in her chair.

Snowball, apparently alarmed by his mistress's loud voice, jumped down and ran out of the room.

"Don't include me. Remember, I'll be going home," Joe told her.

"But you could help us plan this all out," Mandie said.

"Let Jonathan help you plan. He'll be here," Joe said, shrugging his thin shoulders.

"And I will be here, Mandie," Sallie spoke up. "But perhaps we should wait until you talk to Aunt Lou about it before we make any plans. Since she is also the housekeeper of your uncle here, she would know what should be done about it."

Mandie looked at Sallie and smiled. She realized the Cherokee girl was trying to help her smooth things out with the two boys. "You are right, Sallie," Mandie said. "As soon as I can get a chance to talk to Aunt Lou, we will begin making our plans."

"Seems to me y'all are making a mountain out of a molehill," Polly said. "What good will it do y'all to make all these plans and search for the turkey when, if you do find it, it won't be any good by that time and you'll just have to throw it away."

Jonathan immediately looked at Polly and said, "No, no, no! Remember, I told you I would eat it if I find it."

"At least I don't have to plan on eating any of it," Joe said with a smirk.

At that moment Aunt Lou, John Shaw's housekeeper, appeared in the doorway and announced,

"Miz 'Liz'beth say to tell y'all de food be on de table."

As the woman turned to leave, Mandie jumped up to catch her. "Aunt Lou, when they stole the turkey, whoever it was, did they take the pan and the turkey, or just the turkey?"

Aunt Lou stopped to look down at Mandie with a puzzled expression. "'Course dey took de pan, my chile. How else dey gwine carry de turkey off?" she replied.

The young people looked at one another as they followed the woman down the hallway. Aunt Lou went on to the kitchen door and disappeared inside.

"So they did take the pan," Mandie said to her friends.

"And now y'all have to find the pan and the turkey," Joe said with a grin.

"Well, I hope we find them in the same place," Mandie said.

They went into the dining room to join the adults, who were already there. Mandie tried to get her thoughts organized to figure out what they should do next in their search for the missing turkey.

Chapter 2 / Another Discovery

In the dining room Elizabeth Shaw directed the young people to seats at the table, and Mandie found herself sitting between Joe Woodard and her grandmother, Mrs. Taft. Sallie and Polly, with Jonathan between them, sat facing Mandie across the food-laden table.

"Thank goodness the two boys didn't end up next to each other," Mandie said to herself under her breath. She glanced at the adults—Uncle Ned, who was her father's old Cherokee friend and was also Sallie's grandfather, and his wife, Morning Star, Dr. and Mrs. Woodard, and Uncle John Shaw, who had married her mother, Elizabeth, after Mandie's father died.

The adults were already carrying on their own conversation, and Mandie heard Dr. Woodard say, "Yes, 1901 has been a right good year. I hope 1902 is as good or better for us all."

"Shall we give thanks for such a wonderful

year?'' John Shaw asked. ''Uncle Ned, would you return thanks?''

The old Cherokee man nodded and everyone bowed their heads as he spoke. ''Big God, we thank you for being good to us this year past, and we thank you for this good food, and we thank you for the good year coming next. Amen.''

The room buzzed with conversation as food was passed, and everyone began eating. As Mandie always said, ''Mealtime was talking time,'' because that was the time when everyone was settled down together. That was also the time she could sit and listen and learn what was going on. Or she could ask her own questions about things she was interested in. She silently looked around the table and neglected her food.

''Wake up, Mandie!'' Joe suddenly whispered in her ear with a big grin.

Mandie quickly straightened up and gave her attention to her plate. ''I'm not asleep, Joe Woodard. I'm only eavesdropping.''

Joe looked at her in surprise. ''Eavesdropping?'' he asked.

Mandie blew out her breath and said, ''I was only trying to see what our adult guests were talking about, since our younger ones don't seem to be able to carry on a conversation without arguing.'' She took a bite of the potatoes on her plate.

Joe frowned as he leaned closer to Mandie and said, ''Without arguing? I'm sorry, Mandie. I apologize for giving Jonathan such a hard time, but you know he gets to stay here until Monday and I have to leave today and goodness knows what you and he will get into after I've gone.''

Mandie's heart beat faster as she realized that

Joe had not been nice to Jonathan because he was jealous of Jonathan. She laid down her fork and whispered, "Joe Woodard, if you don't want to stay and help unravel the mystery of the missing turkey, that's your hard luck. I'm sure we can do it without you." Suddenly she realized she was too harsh with her lifetime friend. "I'm sorry, Joe. I know you have to leave with your parents, but I just wish you could stay. You and I can solve mysteries much better than anyone else."

Joe reached to pat Mandie's hand that was holding the white linen napkin in her lap as he said with a smile, "I'll do my best to be in on the next mystery."

"Promise?" Mandie asked, withdrawing her hand from his.

"I promise," Joe replied.

"Mandie, what on earth are you and Joe whispering about?" Polly asked from across the table.

Mandie quickly looked at her and said, "Nothing really." She began eating the food on her plate. She saw Sallie smile at her and smiled back.

There was not much conversation throughout the meal until Aunt Lou served the special chocolate layer cake she had baked. Then the young people greedily devoured the pieces on their plates and asked for more.

"Aunt Lou, you shouldn't have baked this cake," Mandie said with a teasing smile.

Aunt Lou immediately stopped passing the cake and asked, "Why, my chile? What's wrong wid it?"

"It's so good there won't be any left for supper," Mandie told her, grinning as she finished the last bite on her plate.

"Dat no trouble, my chile. We'll jes' make another one fo' supper," the old woman told her as she continued passing the cake.

"And I'll be here for supper tonight," Jonathan told her.

"Save me a piece from this cake, and I'll take it home with me for supper," Joe said with a grin.

"Oh, y'all git on now. You's jes' tryin' to pull my leg," Aunt Lou said, shaking her head as she went over to the sideboard to get the coffeepot. She brought it to the table and began refilling coffee cups.

As the old woman paused by her chair, Mandie asked softly, "Aunt Lou, what happened to the turkey? Did you find out anything?"

Aunt Lou looked down at her and said, "Dat turkey, it jes' got up and walked right out of dat oven. Ain't no tellin' whereabouts it went." She refilled Mandie's coffee cup. "Ain't no use you worryin' 'bout it. It's done gone," she added in a low voice.

As Aunt Lou moved on around the table, Mandie noticed her mother looking at her, so she didn't say any more to the old woman.

Joe paused with his fork on the way to his mouth with a bite of ham and whispered, "That's right. It's done gone. So you might as well give up on making a mystery out of it."

"I'm still going to ask Aunt Lou some questions just as soon as I get a chance," Mandie told him.

But later, when Mandie did get an opportunity to question Aunt Lou, she didn't learn anything else. The Woodards had gone home and so had Polly. Sallie and Jonathan stood by listening as Mandie talked to Aunt Lou in the kitchen.

"You didn't hear anything? Or see anybody?" Mandie asked as the young people joined the old woman at the servants' table in the kitchen. Everyone had had their dinner, and the dishes and food had all been cleared away. Aunt Lou was drinking a cup of coffee.

Aunt Lou shook her head and said, "Not a thing. Not a soul. It was jes' like dat turkey jes' 'vaporated in de air, jes' went away all on its own. Didn't nobody hear 'em or see 'em steal it. It jes' disappeared, dat's whut it did."

"Was anything else disturbed?" Jonathan asked.

Aunt Lou frowned at him and replied, "Nuthin' 'cept one of de dishrags. . . . It ain't been found yet."

"So they stole a dishrag, too," Mandie said.

"Mandie, the turkey was hot," Sallie said. "Maybe they used the dishrag to hold the hot pan."

"Uh-huh," Aunt Lou said, nodding her head in agreement. "Dat's whut I'se been thinkin', too." She stood up. "Now I'se got mo' work to do. Off wid y'all." She flapped her big white apron at the young people.

Jonathan and Sallie walked toward the door to the hall. Mandie paused to say, "We'll get that turkey back for you, Aunt Lou."

Aunt Lou replied, "Lawsy mercy, my chile, I don't be wantin' dat turkey back, so don't you bother dat pretty head 'bout it. Wouldn't be no good to eat now nohow."

"We'll see," Mandie said with a big smile as she and her friends went out into the hallway and around a corner, where they settled down on a nearby bench to discuss their plans.

"She's right, Mandie," Jonathan said. "It wouldn't be any good if we found it."

"That's all right," Mandie said. "I'd still like to know what happened to it, and I'm going to find out."

"I will help you discover the turkey," Sallie offered, her multicolored bead necklace swinging as she leaned toward Mandie.

"So will I, for whatever it's worth," Jonathan said.

"Thanks, both of you," Mandie told her friends. "Now, as soon as Aunt Lou comes out of there, we'll search the kitchen."

"If you say so," Jonathan agreed, evidently puzzled by her decision.

"We might be able to find a spot of grease that they might have splattered somewhere, or some dirty footprints, or some sign of whoever stole the turkey from the oven," Mandie explained.

"Or maybe the turkey itself. They might have stashed it away somewhere," Jonathan added. "Like you said before, maybe they were almost caught in the act and had to hide it."

"Yes, that's a good possibility," Mandie agreed. There was the sound of a door opening and closing nearby, and Mandie added, "That's Aunt Lou now. I'll see for sure." She quietly walked over to peek around the corner in the corridor and smiled at her friends as she came back to the bench. "That was Aunt Lou and she went up the back staircase, which means she has probably gone to her room. Come on. Let's hurry."

Jonathan and Sallie followed as Mandie led the way back into the big kitchen. The three quickly opened cabinet doors, drawers, and looked under tables and behind the stove. Snowball was asleep on the woodbox and meowed loudly as his sleep was disturbed. He stood up, stretched, and followed Mandie around the room, still meowing.

"Oh, Snowball, what's the matter with you? Somebody's going to hear you and come to see what's going on," Mandie told the white cat. She opened the door to the large pantry, where dozens of shelves held supplies in jars, bags, boxes, and cans.

Jonathan looked into the room over Mandie's shoulder and asked, "We are not going to look in all those things, are we? That would take forever."

"No, just squeeze the bags and you can tell whether a turkey is in one or not," Mandie told him as she began searching. "The boxes that are sealed don't need to be opened, or the small cans that couldn't possibly hold something as large as a turkey."

"If you will look through the top shelves, I will search the lower ones that I can reach, Jonathan," Sallie said.

"That I will do for you, Sallie," Jonathan replied with a big grin as he began with the top shelf.

They didn't take long to examine everything in the pantry, even though Snowball kept trying to help. He seemed to think they were playing a game and tried to claw the bags until Mandie became aware of his actions and shooed him out of the room. When they finished, the three stood in the middle of the kitchen trying to decide what to do next.

"How far do you think the thief might have been able to go into the house without being seen?" Jonathan asked.

"Probably anywhere in the house except the cellar," Mandie said. "That's kept locked, and I don't imagine he would have had time to unlock the door, go down into the cellar, come back up here, lock the door, and get away."

"Is the cellar locked right now?" Jonathan asked.

Mandie quickly looked at him and realized she had not checked it. "I suppose it is, but I'd better see," she said.

When they checked the cellar door, it was firmly locked. The three wandered on down the corridor to the front hallway and sat down on the bottom step of the main staircase. Snowball followed and curled up on the step above Mandie.

"What's next?" Jonathan asked.

"I'm trying to figure that out," Mandie said. "I'm sure we can't go wandering around the house with all the guests we have here now. My mother wouldn't like it if we snooped in every room."

"Maybe we should go outside?" Sallie asked.

"Outside? Yes," Jonathan said.

"Outside," Mandie repeated. "We could search the yard. There are lots of places out there where a turkey could be hidden." She quickly stood up. "Let's go. But first we need to get our coats."

The three hurriedly retrieved their coats and hats from the hall tree in the front hallway and rushed out into the yard with Snowball close on their heels. They were so wrapped up in solving the mystery of the turkey they didn't even feel the freezing cold weather at first. Only the frozen spots in the dirt bothered them as they almost slipped down when they stepped on one. And a huge icicle fell from the eaves of the roof and barely missed Mandie.

"If we get behind the shrubbery bushes, between them and the house, I don't think any more icicles can hit us if they fall," Mandie told her friends as she pushed the way between two evergreen bushes to get next to the house.

"The bushes are also covered with ice," Sallie remarked as she followed.

"They sure are, and that ice is cold," Jonathan agreed as he made his way after her. Snowball came hopping along on the ice and darted between Jonathan's legs, almost causing him to slide as he tried to dodge the cat. "That cat!" He grabbed at ice-laden branches to keep from falling.

Mandie had turned to look back and saw what happened. "I'm sorry, Jonathan," she said. She held on to a limb and bent to wave one hand at the white cat. "Snowball, go away! Go!"

Snowball looked up at his mistress and meowed loudly. Mandie stomped one foot and said, "Snowball, get!" The white cat retreated a short space and then turned and ran off through the bushes.

"Thanks," Jonathan said, and then with a big grin he added, "That saved him from being stepped on by me."

"Now what we need to do is examine each bush to be sure the turkey is not hidden in the branches," Mandie told her friends.

"With all this ice it would be a frozen turkey if it is," Sallie remarked.

"And I think we're going to be frozen people by the time we put our hands on all these icy bushes," Jonathan added.

"Oh, Jonathan, we all have gloves on," Mandie teased him. She quickly parted the limbs of the bush in front of her to show him how to search. "You just do it real fast like that and your hands will hardly feel the cold."

Jonathan frowned and replied, "I don't believe the turkey could be hidden in any of these bushes anyway. It would be too heavy. It would fall through to the ground if you tried to tuck it away on a limb."

"But some of these bushes are big and have strong limbs," Sallie said. She began looking through the branches of another bush.

"All right," Jonathan said, turning to examine

the shrubbery behind him. "Let's do this fast and get it over with, then."

Mandie secretly smiled at Jonathan when he wasn't looking and led the way on through the bushes around the house. "I'm skipping every two bushes so y'all can look through those."

"What will we do with the turkey if we find it?" Sallie asked as she continued to look through bushes.

"Eat it!" Jonathan said loudly with a big grin as he poked his hands through ice-covered limbs. "After all the trouble that turkey has caused, we would have to eat it and get rid of it for good."

"I'm not sure I would want to eat it. I just want to find out what happened to it," Mandie said.

The three had begun their search with the bushes at the front door and were almost at the back door when Sallie suddenly yelled with her head in the branches of a bush, "I have found something! Wait!" There was something dark green hidden at the trunk of the bush, and she was trying to get it out.

Mandie and Jonathan instantly joined her to help.

"It's a piece of cloth—silk or something," Mandie decided as the object slowly became dislodged from the limb.

Sallie held the fabric tight, stepped back, and pulled. As it came out, she found she had a long dark green silk scarf in her hands. "Look!" she said, holding it up.

"That doesn't look like a turkey to me," Jonathan teased.

"I wonder how that scarf got in that bush and where it came from?" Mandie said as she fingered the silk material.

"It looks expensive," Sallie remarked.

"Are we going to finish searching these bushes or not?" Jonathan asked as he clapped his glove-covered hands together to warm up.

"Of course we are," Mandie replied, but she just stood there holding the scarf up to her nose.

"Then let's get it done," Jonathan said, "so I can go beg a cup of hot coffee from Aunt Lou." He flexed his fingers.

"Are you really so cold?" Sallie asked him.

"Hot coffee would taste good," Jonathan replied.

"All right," Mandie said. "I can't smell anything on this scarf. I thought maybe it might have the odor of the turkey on it if it has been near the turkey." She quickly folded the scarf and stuck it in her coat pocket.

"I don't think that scarf would have been near the turkey. Besides, there's no telling how long it has been in that bush," Jonathan said as they began moving on.

"It had to get there somehow, and I intend finding out how," Mandie replied, reaching into the limbs of the bush in front of her. She realized her hands were getting cold, but she wasn't about to admit it to Jonathan.

The three began moving faster and were soon back around to the front porch, where they had started. Nothing else had been found.

"Now what do we do, Mandie?" Sallie asked as they stopped at the walkway.

"We go beg coffee from Aunt Lou, that's what we do, and I'm going to be the first one there," Jonathan said, and with a big grin he rushed for the front door.

"Yes, I suppose we should stop for now and get warmed up," Mandie agreed as she and Sallie quickly followed Jonathan into the front hallway.

Snowball pushed past the three as he rushed into the warmth of the house.

Mandie removed her coat and hat and hung them on the hall tree and completely forgot about the scarf in her pocket. Jonathan threw his things on a peg and hurried toward the back hallway. Snowball followed.

"I hope Aunt Lou is in the kitchen," Jonathan called back to the girls.

"If she isn't, the coffeepot will be on the stove. It always is," Mandie told him as she and Sallie caught up with him.

"Will Aunt Lou mind if we intrude in her kitchen?" Sallie asked.

"No, she isn't like Jonathan's uppity house-keeper. That woman won't let you near the place," Mandie said with a big smile.

"I've been thinking," Jonathan said, turning back to them. "I wonder if I could persuade Aunt Lou to come to New York and work for us. Then I could go in the kitchen and get food anytime I wanted it." He grinned.

Mandie stopped short and stomped her foot. "Don't go getting any ideas about Aunt Lou. She would never work for a Yankee in that cold place called New York," she said with a big smile.

"Maybe she would for more money," Jonathan continued teasing.

"Uncle John pays her whatever she asks for in wages. Besides, this is her home. She has lived with our family since she was a little girl," Mandie told him. She quickly walked past Jonathan and pushed open the door to the kitchen. She looked around. The room was empty. Snowball rushed over to the warmth of the stove and began washing his face and paws.

"No one here," Jonathan said from behind Mandie.

"But I do see the coffeepot on the stove," Sallie said.

Mandie knew where everything was, and she quickly set down three cups and saucers. Sallie carefully brought the pot of hot coffee from the stove and filled each cup.

"I only want sugar in mine, if you know where it is," Jonathan said as he stood by the table watching the girls.

"It's in the top of that cabinet over there near the stove," Mandie said, indicating a tall cabinet. "And the cream is in the icebox." She crossed the room to open the icebox and take out the cream.

After everything was assembled, the three sat down at the servants' table in the kitchen to discuss the mystery of the turkey and the new mystery of the green silk scarf Sallie had found.

Were the two connected? Did the person who put the scarf in the bush also steal the turkey? Or had there been another mystery concerning the scarf that Mandie had not heard about?

Chapter 3 / Another Mystery

The weather warmed up that afternoon, and the icicles began disappearing. The remaining snow and ice became slushy, and the cold wind died down. But the skies remained cloudy. The three young people had finished their coffee, put the dishes in the sink, and gone to sit in the back parlor.

"I wonder where everyone is?" Mandie said, sitting on a chair near the fireplace. Sallie and Jonathan sat nearby. "I haven't heard a sound since we came back inside."

"They're probably all in their rooms resting for tonight," Jonathan said.

"For tonight?" Mandie asked. "Oh yes, I remember now. They're all going over to the Andersons' for supper. That means we'll have the house all to ourselves, and we can search for the turkey."

"If you say so," Jonathan said with a groan.

"My grandfather and my grandmother will be going over the mountain tomorrow to spend the night with the Witcombs," Sallie remarked.

"But you aren't going, are you?" Mandie asked.

Sallie smiled and said, "No, I told them I would prefer spending time with you. The Witcombs have no young ones in their house."

"I'm glad you aren't going," Mandie said, returning the smile. "We don't get to see each other very often because I'm away in school in Asheville and you live way out at Deep Creek."

"And I live way up in New York," Jonathan said with a loud laugh. "I'm glad you decided to stay here, too, Sallie."

"Yes, I know about New York," Sallie said. "My grandfather told me about his visit to your house when Mandie was there."

"When you stop to think about it, we are all scattered out," Mandie said. "Joe lives in Swain County; Celia in Richmond; Jonathan in New York; and you in Deep Creek, Sallie. And I live here in Franklin and at school in Asheville. Why don't we plan on having a reunion or something, and all of us get together next summer somewhere or other?"

"I vote for Deep Creek. I would like to become acquainted with Uncle Ned's Cherokee family and friends out there," Jonathan quickly told her.

"I would like to visit New York," Sallie said.

"I suppose I would agree to go wherever everyone else wants to, since I've been to all those places," Mandie told her friends.

"I have an idea," Jonathan said. "Why don't I come down here to Franklin when you come home from school for the summer, and we could go visit Uncle Ned. Then we could take Sallie and go to New York to my house?"

"Oh, but you're forgetting Celia," Mandie reminded him, then added, "and Joe."

"All right, then," Jonathan said. "I'll come here after you get home from school this summer. You bring Celia with you. We'll go out to visit Uncle Ned and get Sallie, then we can stop to see Joe and ask him to come along if he wants to. We can all go to my house in New York. Wouldn't that work? Oh, and we could stop in Richmond on the way to New York."

"Whew!" Mandie said, blowing out her breath. "It might take all summer to do that, but we could try. What do you think, Sallie?"

"I believe it would be possible to do all that," Sallie replied.

"Then let's do it!" Jonathan exclaimed.

"We'll have to clear all this with our parents and with Joe and Celia," Mandie reminded him. "But I think they'll all go along with our plans."

"I agree," Sallie said. She smiled at Mandie and then at Jonathan. "This will be an unusual summer for me. I am thankful for friends like you two who brighten up things for my Cherokee people."

"Oh, but, Sallie, please remember I am one-fourth Cherokee, and I claim kinship with the Cherokee people through my father's mother," Mandie reminded her. "I sometimes wonder what would have happened if the white people had not forced the Cherokee people out of North Carolina, because then my white great-grandfather would not have hidden the Cherokee people in his house and my grandfather would not have met my grandmother."

"Oh, Mandie, you are getting too complicated now," Jonathan protested. "None of us would be the person we are now if our parents and grandparents and so forth had not married." Then looking at Sallie, he said, "I would really like to get to know your people and learn their customs and ways."

"Perhaps my grandfather could take you to a council meeting or a powwow," Sallie told him. "He would have to get special permission, since you are white, but he might be able to do that."

"I have been to one," Mandie told Jonathan. "I think I told you about Joe and me discovering that gold, and the Cherokee people had to have a special council meeting to decide what to do with it. But then some of those people are my real kinpeople, you know."

At that moment Mandie looked up and saw Aunt Lou standing in the doorway.

"I'se jes' checkin' to see who bin drinkin' up my coffee," the old woman said.

"We are all three guilty, Aunt Lou," Jonathan told her with a big grin.

"I knows deys three 'cause dat's how many dirty cups in de sink," Aunt Lou said. "I'se jes' checkin' 'cause dem three people dey don't know I'se got 'nother big choc'late cake sittin' in de oven." She started back down the hallway.

"We know now. Thank you, Aunt Lou," Mandie quickly called after her.

"She said she would bake another chocolate cake for supper," Jonathan reminded Mandie. "Do you think she came down here and said that so we'd go back to the kitchen and ask for some?"

Mandie thought for a moment and then said, "It's too close to suppertime. But she knows all the adults will be gone, and it'll be just us eating all that chocolate cake."

"So you plan on eating chocolate cake while the grown-ups are all gone and not searching the house," Jonathan remarked.

"Oh no, I mean, yes, we will search the house. It's just that eating chocolate cake won't take long," Mandie said with a big smile.

Later, soon after the adults had left, Aunt Lou announced supper, and the three made their way straight to the chocolate cake in the middle of the table in the dining room.

Mandie reached for a piece just as Jonathan did, but Aunt Lou was on guard. She swatted at their hands and scolded, "Now y'all gwine eat yo' supper first befo' you gits one bite of dat cake, you hears me?"

"But, Aunt Lou, it would be a nice change if we could just eat dessert first and then eat our supper, don't you think?" Mandie asked with a sly smile as she straightened up in her chair.

"No, dat wouldn't be nice. Things ain't dun dat way in dis heah house, so y'all jes' git busy and eat yo' supper if you wants any of dat cake," the old woman told them with her hands on her ample hips.

At that moment Liza, the young maid, came into the room with a tray full of hot biscuits and cornbread and set them on the table. Mandie quickly looked up at Aunt Lou and said, "Liza can help pass the food, Aunt Lou. You don't have to stay and watch us."

"I knows," Aunt Lou said, folding her arms across her chest as she stood by the sideboard. "And de minute I walks out dat door, dat chocolate cake gwine disappear fast, and Liza won't be sayin' a word to stop you. No, I jes' stays right heah. So go on now and eat yo' supper."

Liza looked from Aunt Lou to Mandie. Mandie knew Liza didn't understand exactly what was going on. But she knew one thing: Aunt Lou was the boss, and whatever she said was the law, so it was either eat supper or do without any chocolate cake.

"I'm starving. Would someone please pass the potatoes?" Jonathan said loudly from where he sat on her right.

Mandie quickly picked up the bowl of potatoes in front of her and gave it to Jonathan. "I'm sorry," she said. Then looking at Aunt Lou, she added, "Aunt Lou, I was mostly teasing you about the chocolate cake. I'm sorry. I do really and truly appreciate all the work you did to bake the cake for us."

"I knows, I knows," Aunt Lou said with a big grin. "I always knows when my chile be serious, and I'm gwine on back to de kitchen 'cause I got things to do back dere. I leave Liza heah wid you, and Liza better do her job right or she gwine heah from me." Turning to Liza, who was standing near her, she said, "Liza, no cake till dey eat their supper, do you heah?"

"Yessum, Aunt Lou, I heahs you," Liza replied. Aunt Lou went out the door, and Liza reached over and picked up the cake. "I'll jes' put it on de sideboard so it won't be no temptation fo' yo' soul, Missy 'Manda." She carried it to the sideboard and set it down by the coffeepot. "Soon as y'all eats, I bring it back, yo' heah, jes' like Aunt Lou said."

"All right, Liza," Mandie agreed as she began putting food on her plate. "We'll eat right fast, and then we'll devour that whole chocolate cake, and then we'll search this house and find that lost turkey." She smiled at Liza.

"And den you'll eat dat turkey," Liza added with a big grin.

"Not me," Mandie said, shaking her blond head. "Jonathan will eat that turkey." She looked at Jonathan and then added as she turned to Sallie, "And Sallie can help him eat it."

"No, Mandie," Sallie disagreed as she began eating the food on her plate. "I do not think I want to eat any of that turkey if we find it. Jonathan can have it all." She smiled at Jonathan.

Jonathan grinned and said, "Sure, I'll eat the whole turkey. It's nice of you girls to give it all to me." He paused and then added, "But I think you agreed on that because you know we'll never find that turkey."

"We won't if we don't ever get finished eating so we can start searching the house," Mandie reminded him. She hastily put a forkful of beans in her mouth.

"Time does fly when one has exciting plans waiting," Sallie remarked. She, too, began quickly consuming the food on her plate.

"Don't forget, we still have that chocolate cake to eat," Jonathan reminded the girls with a big grin. He glanced over at Liza by the sideboard and flashed her a smile.

"Maybe," Liza said teasingly.

When the three had finished the meal, they all decided one slice of cake was enough—for now. They were in a hurry to search the house before the adults returned. They could always eat more cake later, Mandie told Jonathan and Sallie.

For the next hour the three darted in and out of rooms in the huge three-story house, looking under beds, in large drawers, wardrobes, behind furniture, and even in the chimneys of the fireplaces in the rooms that were not being used by guests.

As they finished searching the third floor, Mandie said, "I suppose all that's left is the attic." She looked at her two friends as they stood on the landing of the third floor.

"And that secret tunnel. Don't forget about it," Jonathan reminded her.

"Oh, that tunnel stays locked, and Uncle John has the key, so we'll have to leave that for later, whenever I am able to get the key," Mandie replied. Snowball rubbed around her ankles. The white cat had followed them through the entire search.

"Mandie, do you believe the thief could have gone all the way up to the attic with the turkey?" Sallie asked. "That would have taken time, and the thief would have had to be careful that no one saw him."

"I suppose he could have gone that far from the kitchen," Mandie replied. "Although Liza was working upstairs in the bedrooms when it happened. But then, of course, he could have slipped right by the door of the room she was working in without her seeing him."

"He?" Jonathan asked with a grin. "So you two have decided the thief was a he. I see no reason for that deduction. The thief could very well have been a woman or a girl. No one saw the thief, so no one knows for sure whether the thief was male or female."

"You're right, Jonathan," Mandie agreed. "The thief could have been a woman. But I don't understand why anyone would just walk right into our kitchen and steal a turkey out of the oven, knowing there must be people in the house who might see him or her."

"I have been thinking the reason for the theft must have been hunger," Sallie remarked. "Someone must have been mighty hungry."

"If it was someone really hungry, they should have just asked for food," Mandie said. "I would have given them all the food they wanted if they really needed it."

"Perhaps they had a family at home, maybe little children, and nothing to eat," Sallie said.

"I agree with Mandie that they should have at least asked for it," Jonathan said. "It's not an honest thing to do, going around stealing someone's turkey right out of the oven. And I would say that if the thief was someone who really needed food, then that turkey went straight out the door and to their house. We won't find it in this house."

"Let's go back for more of that chocolate cake," Mandie suggested as she started down the stairs.

"Good idea," Jonathan agreed, following.

"Maybe a small piece of cake," Sallie said, bringing up the rear, with Snowball quickly bouncing down the steps beside her.

When Mandie pushed open the door to the kitchen, she was surprised to see Jason Bond, her uncle's caretaker, sitting at the servants' table, drinking coffee.

"Come in, come in," Mr. Bond greeted them. "I just perked a new pot of coffee on the stove over there."

"Where is everyone? Aunt Lou? Liza?" Mandie asked as she went to the cupboard to get cups and saucers.

"I don't know where they are, but I do know where the chocolate cake is," Jason Bond told her, smiling and pointing across the room. "It's in the pie safe over there. I looked at it and then decided it was too late at night to eat such stuff. 'Course, you might not think it's too late."

"It's never too late to eat chocolate cake," Mandie replied with a big smile. She set the dishes on the table and went to the pie safe. There it was on the middle shelf, and it didn't look like anyone else had eaten any since she and her friends had earlier that night. She took it out and went to set it on the table.

"I will bring the pot and fill the cups," Sallie offered as she walked over to the big iron cookstove and picked up the coffeepot.

"Then I will find the sugar. I think I know where it stays," Jonathan said as he went to the tall cabinet and opened the door. He took out the sugar bowl. "I was right. Here it is." He went to join the others at the table.

"The cake is so sweet I do not want any sugar in my coffee," Sallie told him as he passed the sugar bowl to her. She held the bowl out to Mandie. "Do you want sugar in your coffee?"

Mandie took the bowl and set it down. "No, I agree with you," she said as she picked up the cake knife and began putting slices on the cake plates she had brought from the cupboard.

When they had all settled down with their cake and coffee at the table with Mr. Bond, Mandie asked him, "Do you know about the turkey that was stolen out of the oven today, Mr. Jason?"

"I came in here right after it disappeared, and Aunt Lou was fit to be tied," Mr. Bond said, sipping his coffee.

"Did you see anyone around the house at the time?" Jonathan asked.

"Not a soul," Mr. Bond said. "I was out in the barn repairing a shelf that had started to sag. I didn't see anyone, but then I didn't have a clear view of the back door of the house, either, from there."

"Were you alone? I mean, where was Uncle John and everyone else?" Mandie asked.

"I have no idea, Missy. I didn't see anybody around at all," Mr. Bond replied. "But then with all that ice we had on the ground this morning, I don't suppose anybody would be outside if they didn't have to be."

"We've been searching the house, Mr. Jason, and we haven't found anything that would give us a clue," Mandie said between bites of cake.

"But, Mandie, we did find that scarf outside in the bush," Sallie reminded her.

"Oh yes, I had completely forgotten about that," Mandie said quickly, and turning to Mr. Bond, she explained, "We went outside and searched the shrubbery bushes this afternoon. Sallie found a dark green silk scarf in one of them, but we don't know where it came from, how long it has been there, or even if it is related to the turkey theft."

Mr. Bond looked at her and asked, "You found a silk scarf in the shrubbery? Surely, someone must know they are missing such an item as that. Did you inquire of the ladies if it belonged to them?"

"I plumb forgot about it," Mandie said, shaking her head. "It's still in my coat pocket. But I will ask my mother and all the others about it when they come home tonight."

But Mandie didn't get the opportunity to ask the adults about the scarf that night because they were so late coming home that Mandie and her friends had already retired for the night.

Sallie had the room next to Mandie's room, and they left the door open between the rooms and talked for a while, but Sallie soon drifted off to sleep. Mandie kept thinking about the green scarf, wondering where it came from. Then suddenly she realized she had still left the scarf in her pocket.

"I'd better go get it," she said to herself. She slipped softly out of her bed to go downstairs to the hall tree. Turning back the cover, she pushed Snowball off the bed.

Taking care to be quiet, she walked barefoot down the long hallway and on down the stairs. The lamps along the way were all still lit, which meant that the adults had not returned home. Snowball followed her and began to meow. She quickly picked him up and carried him to try to shut him up. The white cat put his head on her shoulder and hushed.

"Be quiet!" Mandie whispered to Snowball when she reached the hall tree and shifted him to one arm while she reached into the pocket of her coat hanging there. "Wrong pocket, nothing there," she said to herself and then put her hand into the other pocket. "Empty?"

She quickly set Snowball down on the floor and frantically searched both pockets of her coat. The scarf was gone!

"I know I put it in my pocket!" she exclaimed as she bent to search the floor to see if it had somehow fallen out. There was no sign of the green scarf.

"First the turkey disappears and now the scarf disappears!" she muttered to herself. Things were really getting scary. She felt goosebumps run up her arms. "I'll check it out in the morning," she said to herself as she snatched up Snowball and ran back to her room, taking the stairs two at a time.

Chapter 4 / Old Treasures

The next day Mandie was so intent on searching every inch of the house that she forgot about the scarf again. If the turkey was anywhere in the house, she would find it.

"Let's search the attic," Mandie told her friends. The three had gone to sit in the back parlor after breakfast.

"The attic?" Jonathan questioned. "Do you really think someone could have carried the turkey up there?"

"Well, you never know," Mandie replied.

"The attic would be a good hiding place for almost anything," Sallie said. "It is so full of everything."

Mandie laughed and said, "That's right. There's so much stuff up there, you could probably find dozens of places to hide a turkey—pan and all."

Jonathan stood up as he said with a big grin,

46

"Just remember. If we find the turkey up in that dirty attic, I will not eat it."

The girls also rose, and Snowball, lying on the floor beside them, stretched and joined them.

"It's going to be a big job," Mandie warned her friends as they went up the stairs. Snowball followed.

Mandie had searched the attic lots of other times for various reasons. Therefore, she knew most of what the place held. But it seemed like every search uncovered things she had not seen before. And she secretly enjoyed exploring the huge room with its mysterious contents.

Snowball also liked to nose around the place. Sometimes he was a help, and sometimes he was a hindrance. He ran quickly up the steps ahead of his mistress and was waiting when Mandie got to the top and opened the door. Darting around her legs, he disappeared into the piles of boxes, trunks, furniture, and other items stored there.

"Snowball, you don't have to rush so. We have plenty of time to look around this place," Mandie said to the cat as she went over to the windows and opened them in order to get to the shutters outside. When she pushed the shutters back, the outside light illuminated the attic. She pulled the windows back down.

"I suppose the best place to begin would be by the door and then work our way around the room," Jonathan remarked as he stood gazing at the mess.

"It's a big room. There are turns and corners and unexpected hiding places everywhere," Mandie said. "Why don't you start at the door and go to the right, Jonathan, and I could begin there and go to the left. Sallie, you could just go down the middle, or help Jonathan or me."

Sallie smiled and replied, "I will help Snowball. He is sitting there on the trunk in the middle of the floor waiting for me." She walked over to the trunk.

"Are we supposed to open everything—all these boxes and trunks, and furniture with drawers and doors, and all that?" Jonathan asked as he surveyed the conglomeration before him.

"Absolutely everything," Mandie replied. She opened a huge trunk and bent over to look inside. It held old clothes and was only half full. Quickly bending over, she ran her hands through the aged garments and straightened up to close the lid. No turkey in there.

Jonathan was watching her as he stood before an old dresser. "If all you are going to do is open lids and close them, this won't take long," he said.

Mandie looked at him as she went on to another trunk. "That trunk was almost empty and I could see everything in it," she explained. She raised the lid of the trunk before her. "Now, this one is crammed full, so I will have to take enough out to be sure the turkey is not hidden between something." She began pulling old quilts out of the trunk.

"I'll search all the furniture if you will do the trunks," Jonathan said with a big grin as he opened a drawer in the dresser and found it empty.

"Oh no, you have to take whatever you come to on that side," Mandie replied, smiling as she looked at him.

Sallie had stopped examining the contents of the trunk she had chosen and was looking at Mandie and Jonathan.

Mandie shook out a quilt and was about to hang

it across the lid and reach for another one when Sallie suddenly came running across the room.

"Mandie, look at that quilt!" Sallie exclaimed as she came to spread it out.

Mandie looked at the quilt and saw that it was patchworked with lots of symbols of some kind. "This? I wonder what all this means?" she asked in puzzlement as she held one side and Sallie the other.

"It is a Cherokee quilt!" Sallie exclaimed. "It tells a story in our language." She bent over to scan the entire quilt.

"Cherokee?" Mandie asked and then added, "It must have belonged to my Cherokee grandmother. Sallie, what is the story? What does it say?"

Jonathan came to join the girls and inspect the quilt. "Very interesting," he said.

"This would take me some time to understand the story, but my grandfather would be able to read it," Sallie replied, thoughtfully looking at the quilt.

"But he and your grandmother have already gone over the mountain to visit their friends, and they won't be back till sometime tomorrow," Mandie said disappointedly.

"Mandie, that quilt must have been up here for years, so another day or two won't hurt anything to wait for an explanation," Jonathan reminded her.

"I suppose not," Mandie reluctantly agreed.

"Are the other quilts in there made by Cherokee people, Sallie?" Jonathan asked as he looked into the trunk.

"We can look," Sallie said.

"Let's fold this one back up and leave it on the top after we go through the other ones," Mandie said. With Sallie's help she folded it neatly and laid it across the lid of the trunk and pulled out the next one.

Sallie helped stretch the next quilt out and shook her head, "No, this one is not a Cherokee story."

Mandie looked at the many tiny pieces of various cloth material forming the top and said, "No, I suppose someone just used all their scraps to make this one."

"Yes," Sallie agreed. "That is the way some quilts are made. Scraps from everything you make are saved and stitched together."

Mandie quickly pulled out the rest of the quilts, but there was not another one resembling the first. They were all made of scraps, and some had been fashioned into flowers and bows on the quilt tops.

"Let's put them all back in this trunk and leave that special one on top," Mandie told Sallie and Jonathan. "Then when your grandfather gets back, we can ask him to come up here and look at it."

"Why don't you just take it downstairs?" Jonathan asked.

"Because my mother might not like it if I bring things down out of the attic," Mandie told him.

"I suppose you're right. It does really stink," Jonathan said, wrinkling his nose.

"That's the mothballs in this trunk you smell," Mandie explained as she smoothed out the special quilt on top of the stack and closed the lid of the trunk.

"I suppose I'd better get back to work," Jonathan said with a big grin, walking back across the room to the furniture he had been inspecting.

"So should I," Sallie added, going back to the trunk she had been working on.

The next thing on Mandie's side of the room was a huge wardrobe, evidently old and made of solid mahogany. Mandie stooped down to open its big bottom drawer. It was stuck. She sat on the floor, braced her feet against the edges of the wardrobe, and pulled with all her might. It still wouldn't open.

"Oh, shucks!" she exclaimed.

"Need some help?" Jonathan asked, coming over to her. "I've got some drawers over there that are hard to open, too. Move and let me get a hold of that thing."

Mandie moved aside as Jonathan took her place on the floor. He pulled and pulled, but the drawer was still stuck.

Sallie came to join them. "Maybe I can help," she said.

"Jonathan, you pull on the handle on that side, and Sallie and I together can pull on this one," Mandie said. She moved up to grasp the left handle and Sallie reached to help.

"All right, when I say go, pull with all your might," Jonathan told the girls. He caught the handle on the right side with both hands. "Ready?" he asked. Looking at them as they nodded, he said, "Pull!"

The drawer came open with such force that all three young people fell backward, laughing.

Jonathan straightened up to see what they had done. "Look," he said. "The drawer is empty; completely empty. All that work for nothing."

Mandie raised up on her hands and knees to see. "But we wouldn't have known it was empty if we had not got it open," she said.

Sallie started to move forward to join them, then she suddenly stopped. "Look, Mandie!" she exclaimed. "There is something behind the drawer."

"That must be why it was stuck," Mandie said, stooping lower to look into the area behind the open drawer. "Let's pull the drawer the rest of the way out so we can see what's back there."

Once again the three grasped the drawer and pulled. This time it came all the way out of the wardrobe and dropped onto the floor. Mandie lay down and reached into the opening. She felt a lumpy stack of paper and firmly grasped it, then she jerked it until it came free from the frame inside.

"What have you got?" Jonathan asked as Mandie pulled it out.

Mandie looked at the crumbling, yellowed papers in her hand and said, "Looks like a lot of paper, maybe from a notebook or something." She examined it sheet by sheet, carefully turning through it.

"Is it just blank paper?" Sallie asked.

"So far," Mandie replied, continuing to look at the papers.

"I think we should put the drawer back in its proper place," Jonathan said, moving over to the drawer on the floor.

"I will help you," Sallie offered as she joined him. "It is so big it may be hard to put back."

Mandie laid the papers aside on the floor and came to help her friends with the huge drawer. She bent down to look inside. "Can y'all see those runners inside? You know the ones on the bottom of the drawer have to fit those to make it slide back in. Otherwise, if it jumps the track it will stick again," she told them.

Jonathan tilted the drawer to look at the bottom. "Wait," he said, reaching under the drawer. "I believe part of the papers you found are still stuck to the bottom of this drawer." He turned the drawer over on its side.

"You're right!" Mandie exclaimed. She reached for the cluster sticking to the bottom. When she straightened up, she saw that she was holding what looked like the cover of a book and a lot more of the yellowed sheets of paper.

"A diary," Jonathan said with a big grin.

Mandie frowned and looked at him. "It may be a diary, but it's all blank as far as I can tell." She flipped the sheets and suddenly saw faint handwriting on some of them. "No, wait! There's writing here. Look!" She laid the paper out on the floor.

The three crowded around the papers and tried to read the writing.

"It's too dark in here to see this," Mandie said. "Let's go over by the window where the light's better."

They moved across the room, each one carefully carrying part of the papers.

"I still can't read this sheet," Jonathan said, squinting to see.

"I can't read this, either," Mandie said, holding the paper at different angles in the light from the window.

"Neither can I," Sallie said, frowning at the paper she held.

"It's so dark and cloudy outside, it doesn't give much light," Mandie said. "We could light the lamp over there by the door, but I don't think just one lamp would do any good. We need to go downstairs where there's more light."

"And quit our search? That turkey will be rotten

before we ever find it," Jonathan said with a big grin.

Mandie looked around the room. "Why don't we just stack all this paper up by the door over there for the time being and continue our search for the turkey? Then when it's time to eat, we'll have to go downstairs, and we can take the papers with us and look at them down there," she suggested.

"Good idea," Jonathan said.

"Yes, now where do you want us to put these papers?" Sallie asked.

"On that table by the door where the lamp is," Mandie replied, going over to leave the ones she had.

Jonathan and Sallie followed. Just as all the papers were placed on the table, a loud crash on the far end of the room startled all three of them.

"What was that?" Sallie asked, looking around.

"That was whoever this diary belonged to. They don't like it because we are going to read it," Jonathan joked with a grin.

Mandie, drawing a deep breath, said, "Let's just go and investigate." She started in the direction where the sound had come from.

"It's dark over that way. There's no window on that side. Shouldn't we light the lamp and carry it?" Jonathan asked.

"All right, if you say so," Mandie agreed, turning back toward the lamp on the table. She wondered why she had not thought of that. She picked up a match from the box kept on the table and lit the lamp.

"I'll carry it," Jonathan offered as he reached for the lamp.

Mandie handed him the lamp and continued

walking in the direction of the noise they had heard. Sallie followed them. Suddenly it dawned on Mandie that if someone else was in the attic, the lamplight would alert them of their pursuit.

"I don't think—" Mandie started to say in a low whisper to Jonathan, but he suddenly hurried forward with the lamp.

"Look!" Jonathan called back to the girls as he held the lamp high.

Mandie and Sallie hurried to catch up with him. At that moment Snowball came rushing out of the shadows and raced toward the door.

"Snowball!" Mandie exclaimed, stomping her foot. "Snowball has been into something."

"Yes, looks like an old tin bucket full of junk must have fallen from something," Jonathan said, stooping to look at the stuff scattered on the floor by the overturned bucket.

"I should have known when Snowball disappeared he was into something," Mandie said.

The three bent down to pick up the pieces of hardware, nails, and small tools and put them back into the bucket.

"Now let's see if we can get some work done before we have to go downstairs," Mandie told her friends as she started back toward the section she had been searching.

"If we could just go slam, bang, bang around the room, we'd soon get finished," Jonathan suggested.

"What do you mean by that?" Mandie asked.

"You know, just open and close everything real fast instead of bothering to examine everything we find," Jonathan said.

"All right, as long as you don't miss looking into

something," Mandie agreed.

The three continued with their search for the turkey but moved at a faster pace. They went downstairs for the noon meal after washing up enough to be presentable. After they had eaten, they returned to the attic.

By the end of the day, they had more or less skimmed through everything in the attic and went back downstairs again. This time Mandie carried the diary with her. She insisted they should all get cleaned up and put on fresh clothes before the adults saw them. Afterward, they met in the parlor.

The three were gathered around the big open fireplace by the warm crackling fire, discussing their day's work, when Jason Bond came into the room.

"I hear tell y'all been doing a little detective work in the attic today," Mr. Bond said as he sat down nearby.

The three smiled at him, and Mandie said, "But we didn't find the turkey."

"No, I would imagine that turkey is long gone," Mr. Bond said. "But tell me, did you find out who lost that scarf y'all found?"

"The scarf!" Mandie exclaimed. "I forgot all about the scarf! It disappeared!"

"Disappeared? Not the scarf, too!" Jonathan said.

"Yes, it did," Mandie said. "You see, I had put it in my coat pocket when I hung up my coat last night. Then after I went to bed, I remembered it was there. I came downstairs to get it, and it was gone!"

"Are you sure, Mandie?" Sallie asked.

"Maybe whoever it belonged to saw it and took it," Mr. Bond suggested.

"I should have been looking for it today and trying to find out who it belonged to," Mandie said with a deep sigh.

"There are so many things going on, there's no way to keep up with everything," Jonathan said.

"Are you going to ask everyone if they lost a scarf?" Sallie asked.

Before Mandie could answer, Jonathan said, "No, I don't think you should ask anyone about the scarf. We should just listen and see if anyone mentions losing a scarf."

Mandie looked at Jason Bond and asked, "Do you think that's the best way to do it?"

"Maybe," Mr. Bond replied. "If the scarf belonged to whoever took it out of your pocket, I imagine that person would mention to you that they took it."

"Then that's what I'll do," Mandie agreed. "We also found some kind of diary up in the attic. It's old and dirty, so we're waiting till after supper to try to read it."

"A diary? In the attic?" Mr. Bond questioned.

Mandie explained how they had found it. "Do you have any idea as to who might have owned it?"

"Sorry, I don't believe I can help you with that," Mr. Bond said. "From what you say, it might have been up there an awfully long time."

"It's so old the writing is faded, and I doubt that we will be able to read much of it, or maybe none of it," Jonathan said.

"And some of the pages are torn from being stuck behind the drawer," Mandie added.

"I'll take a look at it with y'all if you want," Mr. Bond said.

"As soon as supper is finished, I'll go up and get

it. We'll all meet here in the parlor," Mandie said. "I know that my mother and Uncle John are taking Grandmother and Mr. Guyer to visit some friends after we eat."

"Fine," Mr. Bond agreed.

The three young people discussed the diary all through supper while the adults carried on their own conversation. Mandie was wishing the time away so they could get the papers and see if they could decipher any of the writing. All of a sudden she was getting involved in an awful lot of mysteries, and she needed to solve something or other.

Chapter 5 / Good News, Bad News

As soon as supper was over, the adults left to visit friends, and the young people gathered in the parlor with Mr. Bond. Mandie rushed up to her room, brought the old diary down, and spread the wrinkled and torn sheets of yellowed paper all over the carpet, since there was no table big enough to lay them all out on.

Mr. Bond sat on the floor with Mandie, Jonathan, and Sallie, and they inspected the pages of what had been a book of some kind.

"Let's sort out the ones that don't have anything written on them, and then we can try to read the ones with writing," Mandie said. She began picking up the blank sheets and her friends helped.

"After we take out all the blank ones, there is not going to be much left," Jonathan remarked, adding to the pile in front of Mandie.

"You are right," Mandie agreed. She sat back on her heels and looked at the small stack of papers in front of her. "Now let's divide these and see if we can read any of it." She quickly took several pages off the top and handed them to Mr. Bond, then a few to Sallie, and a few more to Jonathan, leaving a few for herself.

"I need to get under a lamp," Mr. Bond said, rising and going to sit in a chair next to a table with a lamp on it.

"Me too," Jonathan said, and he, too, went to sit by another lamp.

Mandie stood up and said, "Come on, Sallie. We can sit on the settee."

Sallie followed Mandie across the room, and the girls held the papers under the lamp by the settee as they squinted to read the handwriting.

"The only thing I can make out on this page is the word *pig*, and that's in the middle of the scribbling," Mr. Bond announced.

"Pig?" the three young people chorused, looking at the old man.

"That's right, p-i-g," Mr. Bond spelled the word out.

"I can see some numbers on this page," Jonathan told them. He held up the yellowed sheet. "But it's only a number here and there that's legible."

Mandie flipped through the pages she was holding and picked out another one to look at. "A-ha! I've found the word *turkey* at the top of this one," she said excitedly, bending over to look closer.

"Sounds like a farm with pigs and turkeys," Jonathan joked.

"You are right, Jonathan," Sallie said. She looked up from the sheet she was examining. "I can see the word *farm* right in the middle of this one."

"Well, of course, all this land around here used

to be farmland and the Shaw family," Mr. Bond told them. "That was many years ago, and these papers look like they were written many years ago."

Mandie looked at him and asked, "Do you think this was some kind of record book for the farm then?"

"Maybe," Jason Bond replied. "You might ask your uncle John to look at these papers. Perhaps he could figure out what they are."

Mandie drew a deep breath and said, "Oh, shucks! I already need Uncle Ned to look at that quilt we found in the attic, and he's gone for the night. Now I need Uncle John to look at these pages, or book, or whatever you call it, and he probably won't be back with my mother and the others until we have gone to bed."

"A quilt you found in the attic?" Jason Bond asked. "I know there must be dozens of quilts in trunks and drawers in the attic. Did y'all find a special one of some kind?"

"Yes, sir," Mandie replied. "Sallie said it was a Cherokee quilt. It was in a trunk with a lot of other quilts, but it's completely different, isn't it, Sallie?" She looked at her friend.

"Yes, it has Cherokee symbols and tells a story, but I cannot read it. My grandfather can interpret the meaning," the Cherokee girl replied.

"Since your father's mother was Cherokee, Amanda, and she lived here, there may be lots of things associated with her people stashed away in the attic," Jason Bond told Mandie.

"So you think the quilt belonged to her?" Mandie asked.

"Could be," Jason Bond replied. "But when you get Uncle Ned to translate the message on the quilt, you may know more about it, I'd say."

Mandie sighed deeply. "We are finding so many mysteries and then not being able to follow through with anything. It's frustrating."

"Yes, and you may have run into one too many mysteries to solve," Jonathan teased. "I believe I count four—the turkey, the scarf, the quilt, and the torn-up book. You do have to go back to school next week, and we do have to go home soon."

"Oh, never you mind," Mandie said with a shrug. "We'll solve all four. You wait and see." She was secretly wondering how they would ever be able to accomplish all this, but she would never let Jonathan know this.

The young people stayed up late that night. Mandie was hoping the adults would return before they went to bed, but no such luck. At the stroke of midnight, the three finally retired. They had not been able to read any more of the faded writing, and Mandie took the papers back to her room and put them on her bureau. First thing in the morning she would show them to her uncle John and ask if he knew what they were.

But the first event the next morning, which was Saturday, was a disappointment. When Mandie and Sallie went downstairs with Jonathan for breakfast, Aunt Lou, the housekeeper, was waiting to serve their breakfast. Otherwise the room was empty.

"Y'all chillun, jes' git to de table now and I bring de food," the old woman told them as she bustled about with dishes on the sideboard.

Mandie stopped to look at her and asked, "Where is everyone else? Are we late?"

"No, my chile," Aunt Lou replied, setting a plate filled with ham on the table. "Ain't nobody but y'all a-comin' to eat dis mawnin'.''

"Why?" Mandie asked in surprise. She and her friends sat down at the linen-covered table.

"Well, fust of all, Mistuh John took dat Mistuh Guyer off some place to see 'bout buyin' a mine or somethin' like dat," Aunt Lou explained.

Jonathan quickly interrupted, "My father is going to buy a mine? What kind of mine?"

"I don't be knowin'," Aunt Lou replied. She brought the coffeepot from the sideboard and filled their cups. "Alls I knows is whut Mistuh John say to me dis' mawnin' when dey leave. He say, 'We's gwine find a mine fo' Mr. Guyer to buy and we may be gone a few days.' "

"A few days?" Mandie repeated in disappointment. "I need to talk to him about something. Oh, shucks!"

"And den dis heah Injun man he come a-knockin' at de back do' soon as Mistuh John and Mistuh Guyer leaves and he say Uncle Ned and Mawnin' Star send word dey don't be comin' back till mebbe Sunday night or mebbe Monday mawnin'," the old woman explained. "And Miz 'Liz'beth and Miz Taft dey sleepin' late 'cause dey out late last night. And Mr. Bond he dun went on a errand."

"My grandfather had said we would go home Sunday," Sallie remarked.

"My father and I are supposed to leave Monday," Jonathan said.

"Oh well, y'all just get to stay a little longer," Mandie reminded her friends.

"Y'all eat up now, you heahs?" Aunt Lou told the young people. She stood by the sideboard watching. "Dat white cat he be in de kitchen already eatin' his breakfast."

"That's his favorite room in this house," Mandie said as she began eating the bacon and eggs on her plate.

"So what are we going to do today?" Jonathan asked. He reached for a hot biscuit and buttered it.

"We still haven't found the turkey," Mandie reminded him.

Sallie took a sip of her coffee and said, "We have searched everywhere for the turkey. What do you plan to do about it now?"

"We still have the cellar to search," Mandie reminded her friends with a mischievous grin on her face.

"That dark and spooky underground cavern," Jonathan teased.

At that moment Mandie heard a loud knock at the front door. Before she could decide who it was, Liza, the young maid, came to the doorway of the dining room with Dr. Woodard and Joe.

"We'se got mo' comp'ny," Liza announced as the Woodards stepped inside the room.

Aunt Lou quickly took over. "Liza, get two mo' plates," she said. "And, Doctuh, y'all jes' go ahead and sit down."

"Well, I'm glad to see y'all back, but it's a big surprise," Mandie said.

Dr. Woodard and Joe pulled out two chairs and sat down at the table.

"And it's a big surprise to us, too," Joe replied with a big grin. He looked at his father.

Dr. Woodard smiled at him and said, "Go ahead and tell them the news. It's all yours, son."

Mandie was impatiently waiting for an explanation.

Joe looked around the table, and his gaze settled on Mandie as he began. "It's good news, but it's also bad news." He paused.

"Joe Woodard, tell us what's going on. We're about to ask your dad if you don't," Mandie told him, pretending to be exasperated.

"All right, to make it short, I'm going away to college. I've been accepted—" Joe was interrupted by all three young people.

"College?" Sallie asked.

"Where?" Mandie demanded.

"So you made it," Jonathan said.

"Yes, I made it. And the where is New Orleans," Joe replied to Mandie's question. "That's—"

Mandie quickly interrupted again. "New Orleans? That's all the way down in Louisiana," she said.

"It sure is," Joe agreed with a big smile.

"Do you have to go that far away?" Mandie asked with a slight catch in her voice as her blue eyes suddenly filled with tears. She dropped her gaze and pretended to have swallowed wrong, holding her napkin up to her face to secretly dab at the tears.

"It's not all that far away by train. All of you can come down and visit and see the college," Joe insisted.

"Yes, I'd like to visit down there," Jonathan agreed.

"I would like to go, too," Sallie added.

Mandie finally looked back at Joe and asked, "Did you come all the way back here just to tell us you're going away to college?"

"Oh no," Joe said, picking up the cup of coffee Liza placed by his plate and sipping from it. "We really had two reasons. My father has some patients over here, and he wanted to check on them before we leave. Then he is getting the train with me from here to go to New Orleans. But—" he paused slightly, "my own personal reason was to come and tell you in person, Mandie."

Mandie quickly blinked her blue eyes to clear her vision. "Thank you, Joe," she said in a small voice. "I'm going to miss you. After all, you've been around all my life."

"Of course, I'll miss you, all of you, too, but in order to get an education, I have to go away," Joe said with a frown.

Dr. Woodard cleared his throat, put down his fork, and said, "We are all going to miss Joe, but, Miss Amanda, you will be going off to college one day in the near future, too, and we're going to miss you. When you young people have completed your education, I hope you will come back here."

"Oh, I will, Dr. Woodard," Mandie agreed quickly. "If there was any way to keep from ever leaving here at all, I would stay here forever."

"And I suppose I'll live in New York forever," Jonathan said. "After being sent all around the world to boarding schools, I don't want to leave home ever again. So I know how you feel, Mandie."

"And I will stay with my people forever, except for the opportunity to get a good education," Sallie remarked.

"I'm glad you came back," Mandie told Joe.

"When we got home, we found the acceptance letter in the mailbox, and the first thing I thought of was that I have to tell Mandie," Joe explained with a teasing grin. "Otherwise you might try to make a mystery out of it."

Everyone laughed, and the sad feeling left Mandie as she said, "I'm sure there must be mysteries down there in New Orleans, so I might just show up at your door one of these days." She laughed.

"Come ahead," Joe said, then looking around he added, "All of you. I can't guarantee you what kind of place I'll be living in, since I've never been there."

"Never been there? You mean you're going to a college you haven't even seen?" Jonathan asked.

"How did you get accepted?" Mandie asked.

"I suppose I'd better explain," Joe told them. "You see, I had applied to several colleges through the mail, and my father and I had visited two of them, but they weren't what I was looking for. Then our schoolteacher, Mr. Tallant, heard that I was looking. He himself went to this college and he recommended me. They allowed him to give me the examinations necessary for consideration."

"Finish your story, son," Dr. Woodard said, smiling at Joe.

"Well . . ." Joe dragged out the word.

"Then I will finish it," Dr. Woodard said, looking around the table. "Joe came out in the top ten percent of several hundred students taking the examinations for entrance."

Mandie quickly clapped her hands, and Jonathan and Sallie followed.

"I'm not surprised. I'm proud to have known you, Joe Woodard," Mandie said in a shaky voice.

"To have known me? Why, I still know you," Joe teased.

"Oh, I have a wonderful idea!" Mandie exclaimed. She looked at Sallie and Jonathan and said, "We should give him a going-away party!"

"Yes!" Jonathan agreed.

"Of course," Sallie said.

"Now, when do you have to leave on the train?" Mandie asked.

"This coming Tuesday," Joe replied. "But you don't have to get up a party for me."

"Tuesday is the last day of this year," Mandie said. "I suppose we'll have to have the party on Monday night. I do hope Uncle Ned and Morning Star get back in time." She looked at Sallie and then Jonathan as she added, "And your father and Uncle John."

"Are they all gone somewhere?" Dr. Woodard asked.

"Yes, sir," Mandie said and explained where everyone was. "My mother and grandmother should be down soon. Aunt Lou said they're sleeping a little late because they were out late last night."

Liza, the maid, had been standing by the sideboard listening to the conversation. Aunt Lou had left the room.

"Missy 'Manda, kin I be he'pin' wid dat party?" Liza asked in a whisper across the room.

"Of course, Liza," Mandie told her. "You and I could go to the store for a few things that we'll need for the party."

"Yessum, Missy 'Manda, dat be a good idea," Liza said, smiling big.

"I suppose y'all have solved the mystery of the missing turkey by now," Joe remarked as he looked around the table.

"Not yet," Jonathan said.

"But we've been working on it. You can help us finish our search. All we have left is the cellar," Mandie told him.

"You don't really believe that turkey could be in the cellar, do you?" Joe asked.

"There's a possibility it could be, and we won't know until we do search the place down there," Mandie told him. "Are you going to help us?"

"I suppose I could go along and hold the lamp or something," Joe said with a big smile.

"And help me protect the girls from the spooks down there," Jonathan teased as he looked at Joe.

"Jonathan!" Mandie protested.

At that moment Mandie's mother and grand-mother came into the dining room, followed by Aunt Lou, who was carrying clean dishes to set places for them on the table.

"Well, good morning, Dr. Woodard. It's nice to see you again," Elizabeth told him as she and Mrs. Taft sat down at the table.

"Thank you, Elizabeth. I appreciate your open hospitality," Dr. Woodard replied. "We had to make a return trip here to catch the train and tie up some loose ends with patients." He explained their reasons.

"I know you're proud of Joe," Mrs. Taft said.

Joe quickly looked at the adults and said, "Could I be excused please? We have to search the cellar." He rose. "The turkey is still missing."

The other young people followed, and they hast-ily left the room as the adults began discussing the missing turkey. Mandie led the way to the wide staircase in the front hallway, where they all sat on the steps and planned their trip into the dark and mysterious cellar.

Mandie explained to Joe about the quilt and the old book they found in the attic. "So you see, we have more than just the fate of that turkey to solve."

"I'd like to see the book," Joe said.

"It's not exactly a book," Mandie explained. "It probably was a book at one time, but now it's just a lot of loose paper, all dirty, torn, with the handwriting all but evaporated."

Jonathan stood up. "What do you say we get on with this job in the cellar so we can get ready for the party?" he asked.

"Let's get some lamps from the back hallway," Mandie said, rising to lead the way.

"And plenty of matches," Joe added. "We have been known to have lamps go out and no matches to relight them."

"That wouldn't be too good in that dark cellar," Jonathan said.

"Don't worry," Mandie told her friends. "I'll bring plenty of matches."

Mandie was anxious to complete the search and get started on the preparations for the party. That would be special because there was no telling how long it would be before Joe came back to visit. She was already missing him.

Chapter 6 / Secret Plans

The cellar was not as hard to search as the attic. Everything was in neat rows on shelves up to fifteen feet high and with proper labels.

Mandie led the way down the steep stairs from the back hallway, holding a lighted lamp up high to illuminate the way. The others followed with more lamps.

"Please don't move anything out of order," Mandie told her friends. "This is Aunt Lou's domain, and just recently she had everyone down here cleaning, labeling, and stacking everything. It's all right to move things to look behind them, but please put everything back exactly the way it was."

"Yes, ma'am," Jonathan said with a mischievous laugh. "Anything else, ma'am?"

Mandie turned back to look at him and said, "Yes, watch out for snakes and spiders. Plenty of those things live down here."

"Jonathan, you and I could search the top

shelves, and the girls could look at the lower ones they can reach," Joe suggested, looking around.

"Right," Jonathan agreed. He started toward the far end of the huge room. "I'll begin at this end, and you start back there, and we'll eventually meet."

"Sallie, let's you and I just work together," Mandie told her friend. "That way we can take turns holding the lamp while the other one searches."

"That is a good idea," Sallie agreed.

But searching through the cellar didn't turn out to be a good idea. All that work, and they didn't find a single clue to the mystery of the missing turkey. All they accomplished was to get so dirty they had to go to their rooms, clean up, and change clothes. And they were almost late for the noon meal.

During the conversations at the table, Mandie kept in the back of her mind that she needed to speak to her mother about having a party for Joe, but she couldn't do it with Joe around. So when the meal was over, Mandie waited until her mother and her grandmother had gone to the parlor and the young people were standing around in the hallway.

"Why don't y'all sit down on the steps there and wait for me? I have to see my mother about something," Mandie told her friends.

"Go right ahead, Mandie. We will wait for you," Sallie told her.

The boys agreed, and the three drifted over to the stairs and sat down.

Mandie found her mother and grandmother both reading in the parlor. She smiled as she entered the room. "Those must be awfully interesting books for y'all to get back to them so soon after we ate."

"Yes," both women said.

Before they could say any more, Mandie told her mother, "I want to ask your permission to give Joe a going-away party. And we need to do it on Monday night because he and his father are leaving Tuesday."

Elizabeth looked at her and said, "That's a thoughtful idea, dear. Now, what do we need to do to get things started?"

"I'd like to decorate the back parlor and keep the door closed until time for the party so it will be a surprise to Joe," Mandie replied. "And I'd like to ask Aunt Lou to bake a huge chocolate cake, which is his favorite."

"Fine," Elizabeth agreed.

Mrs. Taft looked up from her book and said, "Maybe we ought to give him going-away presents. What do you think?"

"Oh, Grandmother, that's a great idea!" Mandie agreed. "Liza asked me this morning if she could help if we have a party, so I thought Sallie and I could take Liza to the store and buy a few things while Jonathan keeps Joe occupied."

"Would you mind shopping for me?" Mrs. Taft asked her. "Get him something that you think he would like and wrap it up for me. Of course, I'll give you money to spend in the store."

"Yes, that's a good idea. You know better than we do what Joe likes, so I'll let you get something from me to give him, too," Elizabeth said. Looking at her mother, she said, "You don't need to give Amanda any money. We have an account at Stovall's Store, so she can just get whatever we need from there. They do have a big variety of merchandise."

"All right," Mrs. Taft agreed. "You and I can settle the bill afterward."

"Mother, I do hope Uncle John and Mr. Guyer get back in time for the party, and Uncle Ned and Morning Star, too. Everyone would have to be gone somewhere," Mandie said.

"I'm sure they will all be back by Monday night, dear," Elizabeth assured her.

Mandie thought about the old book and the quilt they had found in the attic and would have liked to discuss it with her grandmother, who was old enough to remember the Shaw family who had farmed the land. But right now she just didn't have time to talk about it. Maybe later she would have the opportunity.

"Thanks, Mother," Mandie said. "I'll go talk to Aunt Lou, and then Sallie and Liza and I will go to the store."

As she passed the staircase, she found Sallie and Jonathan waiting there. She stopped to whisper, "Where is Joe?"

"He went to his room for a minute," Jonathan told her.

At that moment the three heard footsteps on the stairs above.

"He's coming down now," Mandie whispered quickly. "Jonathan, please keep him occupied while the rest of us get the party planned. Sallie, come with me, and we'll get Liza and go to the store."

"How am I supposed to keep him occupied?" Jonathan asked.

"Mother and Grandmother are in the parlor. Ask them if you and Joe can play a game on Uncle John's chess set, or checkers, or something, just anything," Mandie quickly told him as she rushed down the hallway toward the kitchen with Sallie following.

When Mandie pushed open the door to the kitchen, Snowball, her white cat, rushed out into the hallway and raced off toward the parlor. Aunt Lou, Liza, Jenny, the cook, and her husband, Abraham, were all sitting at the table drinking coffee.

"Guess what? Mother has agreed that we can give Joe a going-away party," Mandie told them. She and Sallie walked over and sat on empty chairs.

"I s'pose we'se gwine make a chocolate cake," Aunt Lou said with a big smile.

"Right," Mandie agreed. "And, Aunt Lou, could we plan this so we have supper like usual in the dining room, but you don't give us any dessert? Then when everyone is finished, I will delay Joe from leaving the room and give everyone time to get into the back parlor. Then I will talk about something or other and ask him to come on to the back parlor. I will tell him that that's where Sallie and Jonathan went, or some such story."

"Dat'll work jes' fine, my chile," the old woman agreed.

"Between now and Monday night we need to keep that parlor door closed so we can decorate without him seeing it," Mandie added.

"And we has to keep him out of heah, too, 'cause he might see de cake," Jenny said.

"Gwine miss dat boy. He good boy," Abraham remarked while he drank his coffee.

"We's all gwine miss him, but he gotta do dis so he kin be eddicated when he gits to be a lawyer man," Aunt Lou said. "And den one day my chile be gwine off to dat faraway school and we sho' nuff gwine miss huh.''

Mandie quickly reached out and hugged the big woman. Aunt Lou squeezed her tight.

''I may have to go away now and then for a while, but you can count on me always coming back,'' Mandie assured Aunt Lou. She looked at the other servants to include them as she straightened up.

''And I knows dat Uncle Ned gwine miss his lil' granddaughter here when she grow up and go away,'' Aunt Lou said, reaching to embrace Sallie.

Sallie smiled up at her and returned the hug.

''Maybe Sallie and I will be able to go to the same college,'' Mandie said.

''That is a perfect idea, Mandie,'' Sallie agreed. ''I will speak to my grandfather about it.''

''So will I,'' Mandie replied, and turning back to the servants, she asked, ''Aunt Lou, would it be all right if we took Liza to the store with us right now? We won't be gone long.''

''Go right ahaid, my chile, take Liza,'' the old woman said, and turning to Liza, who had not said a word yet, she added, ''And, Liza, you behave yourself, you heah?''

''Yessum, I heahs,'' Liza said with a big smile for Mandie.

''Does you need me to take y'all in de buggy?'' Abraham asked.

''No, thank you, Abraham. We can walk. It's not all that far, and the weather has turned warmer,'' Mandie said. ''Thanks anyway. If y'all would just keep this a secret in case Joe wanders back here, I'd appreciate it.''

The servants promised, and the girls went to get their coats and hats.

Stovall's Store was the largest store in Franklin and also had the largest selection of merchandise, everything from jewelry to clothes to washtubs to cookstoves. It was Saturday, so the place was crowded. The girls moved around through the crowd and examined the merchandise as they went.

Mandie stopped to look at the knives. "I think maybe a nice knife from Mother and Uncle John would do. And I could buy a shoeshine set for Grandmother to give him." She paused to think and then added, "I will give him a book to keep a daily journal."

"I will ask my grandfather to give him one of his arrows," Sallie said. "Joe has always admired them."

"Oh, Sallie, that will be the best present of all. He'll treasure that," Mandie assured her. "Now, Liza, since you came with us and you are helping, why don't we get one of those leather straps over there to carry his books?"

Liza's eyes widened as she looked at the straps. "Does you think I could really give him one of dem?"

"Sure, they don't cost much. I'll just add it on our bill today, and I'm sure it will be all right with Mother," Mandie told her.

"Oh, Missy 'Manda, I sho' does thank you, and I think he sho' gwine like it," Liza said, fingering the rack of belts.

"When Dr. Woodard comes back to our house, I'll ask him if Joe needs one," Mandie told Liza, "but I'm sure he does, so you go ahead and pick one out while I go over to get a shoeshine set. Stay right here so we won't lose you." She turned to go back down the aisle they had come up and almost collided with a man. "I'm sorry," she muttered, but the man didn't even acknowledge her as he continued on his way. He was a tall, heavyset man with a beard and was wearing old gray workclothes with a black patch on one knee. She had never seen him before.

"Did you see that man?" Mandie asked Sallie. "We almost knocked each other down, and he didn't say a word. Do you suppose he's deaf?"

"But, Mandie, even if he is deaf, he could see that he almost bumped into you," Sallie replied, looking back at the man, who disappeared in the crowd.

"You're right. Oh well," Mandie said as she walked on down the aisle. She thought about the man while she looked at the shoeshine sets. He had been just plain rude, she decided, and if she saw him again she would tell him so.

"I believe this one, with everything in it, would be what Grandmother would want me to buy," Mandie said to Sallie, holding up a box that contained polish, brushes, shine rags, and even an extra pair of shoelaces.

"Yes, that one would be special," Sallie agreed.

Mandie carried the box with her and said, "Let's go get that knife for Mother and Uncle John to give him, and I believe I saw the books near that counter."

Mandie selected the most expensive knife in the counter and then made her way through the crowd to the stacks of books. Sallie followed.

"I think Joe would like this one," Mandie said to Sallie as she flipped through the pages of a journal. Looking on to the next section of the store, she added, "And you know, Sallie, we should get some of that lace and ribbons and paper over there and make some little fancy decorations."

"We could use some of the straw in your uncle's barn with that lace and ribbons and create little people and animals," Sallie suggested.

"Oh yes, let's do," Mandie agreed as they moved on toward the ribbon counter. Her arms were full with the shoeshine box, the knife, and the book, and she looked around. "I wonder where Liza is. I need her to hold these for me while I pick out the ribbons and lace."

Sallie reached for the purchases and said, "I will hold them for you, Mandie. Liza must still be selecting a strap for Joe's books."

Mandie handed her the items and said, "Surely she is not taking all this time for that. We'll go back and find her as soon as I get this done." She turned to the rows of bright ribbons and dainty laces.

Mandie and Sallie found Liza still standing there sorting through the book straps. She would look at one and then another.

"Liza," Mandie said. "Have you picked one out yet?"

The young girl shook her head and said, "Ain't niver had to pick sumpin' out befo'. Don't know how to do it, Missy 'Manda." She looked thoroughly confused.

Mandie compressed a smile and explained, "Liza, you just look at the straps and think which one Joe would like."

"Now, how does I think dat?" Liza asked.

"You imagine. You know, like you're making up a story. You just imagine seeing Joe with his books held together by one of these," Mandie replied.

"But, Missy 'Manda, I ain't niver seed Joe with no book," Liza told her.

Mandie frowned and said, "I suppose you're right. When Joe comes to see us, he doesn't have his schoolbooks with him. Let's do it this way. Suppose you had a stack of books to carry. Which strap do you think would look nice around them and would hold the books together better?"

"In dat case, Missy 'Manda, I'd say dis heah one de best," Liza told her as she pulled out a wide belt from the display rod.

Mandie took it and agreed. "Yes, I believe this one would be what Joe would like. Now let's take all these things over to the counter so they can be put on Uncle John's account."

The girls finally got finished in the store and started the walk back to the house. They made their plans as they went.

Back at the house everyone seemed to have disappeared. No one was in the parlor, and no one was in their bedrooms. Mandie went to the kitchen to see if the servants knew where her mother and grandmother and the boys were. Sallie and Liza followed.

"Why dat Miss Polly she come over heah right aftuh y'all left, and when she finds y'all not heah, she tell Miz 'Liz'beth dat she go home. And Miz 'Liz'beth she say do de boys want to go visit Miss Polly's house, so next thing I knowed, dey all left and went next do'," Aunt Lou explained.

Mandie looked at Sallie and said, "Mother must have done that so we could get back in without Joe seeing what we bought."

"Yes," Sallie agreed.

"Has Dr. Woodard come back from making his calls?" Mandie asked.

"No sign of him yet," Aunt Lou told her.

"We took everything we bought up to my room," Mandie told the woman. "We could start making the decorations while they're gone. We need some needles and thread, scissors and pins and a tape measure."

"Liza know where to find all dat," the woman said. Turning to the young girl, she said, "Liza, you go up to my sewing room and find all dis heah stuff. You knows where I keeps it. Now, off wid y'all. I got to get supper going heah." She turned to the big iron cookstove.

"Thanks, Aunt Lou," Mandie called back to her as she, Sallie, and Liza left the kitchen.

Walking down the hallway toward the staircase, Mandie said, "You might know Polly Cornwallis would find out that Joe is back. Now she'll be hanging around in our way while we're trying to decorate the room for the party."

"Not if she is trying to keep up with Joe because Joe will not be with us when we decorate," Sallie reminded her.

Mandie frowned and said, "I don't know how that will work out. She'll be trying to find out what we're doing, and she'll also be trying to follow Joe around."

"What will Joe think if we just disappear into another room while he is in the house? Will he think we are trying to avoid him?" Sallie asked as the three girls climbed the stairs.

"We will probably have to decorate the room at night after he goes to bed," Mandie suggested.

"I stay up late and he'p," Liza offered.

When they got up to Aunt Lou's sewing room, Mandie looked around and said, "Why don't we just

work in here? It's far enough away from the bedrooms that no one would see or hear us.''

"That would be the best thing to do,'' Sallie
agreed.

"I git de stuff we bought and bring it to dis
room,'' Liza said, turning toward the door.

"We'll all go, Liza,'' Mandie said.

They had just managed to get the things into
Aunt Lou's sewing room when they heard the boys
down the stairs.

"They're back. We'd better go join them so they
won't look for us,'' Mandie said.

"They might think we are still looking for the turkey,'' Sallie said as they descended the staircase.

"That turkey bothers me. We still ought to
search for it,'' Mandie said.

"But where, Mandie?'' Sallie asked.

"I'll have to think about it and decide later,''
Mandie told her. Somehow she was going to find out
where that turkey went.

Chapter 7 / When Will the Mysteries End?

Halfway down the staircase Mandie and Sallie met Joe and Jonathan coming up the steps. The four of them paused to ask questions.

"Well, where did you two go?" Jonathan asked.

"I'd like to know where you two have been," Mandie said with a little smile.

"We went over to Polly's house with your mother and your grandmother," Joe told her.

"Did my mother and grandmother come back with y'all?" Mandie asked.

Snowball came racing up the steps to his mistress. He rubbed against her legs and meowed loudly. Mandie ignored him, so he sat down and began washing his face.

"No, they said they'd be on in a few minutes. Mrs. Cornwallis wanted to show them a new dress she had made," Joe explained.

"Did you find that turkey while we were gone? I sure am hungry," Jonathan teased.

"Do you mean Polly didn't serve y'all afternoon tea? She tries to be so proper you'd think she would offer y'all refreshments," Mandie said with a big smile.

"Well, you see, when the maid was told to bring in the tea, Joe and I decided it was a good time to escape," Jonathan replied, glancing at Joe with a grin.

Joe added, "Besides, we figured Aunt Lou would be feeding you girls some of her gooey, delicious chocolate cake." He looked at Sallie and asked, "Y'all didn't eat it up, did you?"

"No, Joe, we have not had one bite of Aunt Lou's chocolate cake," Sallie replied, looking at Mandie. "I am not sure that she has a chocolate cake."

Mandie quickly said, "We haven't even asked if Aunt Lou had any chocolate cake for us this afternoon."

"What have you been doing if you haven't had time for cake?" Jonathan teased. "Been looking for that turkey again?"

Mandie frowned and said, "Actually, I've been trying to decide where we should look next."

"Mandie, there is no other place to look," Joe told her.

"Maybe if we all keep thinking about it, we can come up with someplace to search," Mandie said.

"What about the scarf we found that disappeared?" Jonathan asked. "We still don't know whose scarf it was. And we still have to ask Uncle Ned about that quilt you found in the attic."

"Whenever my grandfather returns, either Sunday night or Monday morning, he will read the quilt for Mandie," Sallie said.

"And don't forget about that torn-up book we found," Mandie reminded her friends. "We still don't know anything about it." She frowned and drew a deep breath. "If everybody hadn't decided to run off somewhere, we could solve at least two of the mysteries, the quilt and the book."

"But, Mandie, we are not sure your uncle will know anything about the book," Sallie told her.

"Maybe we should start snooping into everyone's rooms and see if we can refind that green scarf," Jonathan suggested with a mischievous grin.

"Oh no, we couldn't do that!" Mandie exclaimed. "My mother would be madder than an old wet hen. We would be in deep trouble. Why don't we just go in the parlor and sit by the fire while Joe tells us about his college?"

"Yes," Sallie agreed.

"That would be more interesting than trying to solve these mysteries that have no solutions," Jonathan joked.

"Ah, but Mandie can always find a mystery, and I don't know of a single one she hasn't been able to unravel," Joe said, smiling at Mandie.

"That's because there's always an answer to a mystery if you keep at it long enough," Mandie said with a smile of satisfaction as she led the way down the hallway to the parlor.

Snowball raced ahead and hurried to curl up on the warm hearth. Mandie and her friends sat down close by.

"Tell me one thing, Joe," Jonathan began. "How did you happen to start college at midyear?"

"That's because I need to catch up on some studies that Mr. Tallant didn't teach. My first half year will be for that. Then in the fall I will begin the first full-length year," Joe explained.

"I never heard of anyone doing that before. I always thought you had to have already had the required subjects before the college would admit you," Jonathan replied.

"You still do. The college is allowing me to do this because of Mr. Tallant's recommendation and because he does not teach what I need," Joe said.

"That must be partly because of the high score your father said you made on the examinations," Mandie said.

Joe squirmed around in his seat. He was never comfortable with compliments. "I suppose so," he said.

At that moment Mandie heard the front door open and voices in the hall. Her mother and grandmother had returned, and it sure sounded like Polly with them. In a moment the three of them appeared in the doorway to the parlor.

"Polly will be staying for supper, dear," Elizabeth said. "Has your father returned from his calls, Joe?"

"No, ma'am," Joe replied.

Polly entered the parlor and sat down in a chair next to the settee where Joe and Jonathan were sitting.

"We're going on up to our rooms," Mrs. Taft told them. "We'll be back down in time for supper."

"That won't be long," Mandie called to the two women as they went on down the hallway.

"What did y'all buy at the store?" Polly asked Mandie.

"The store?" Mandie questioned.

"Your mother told my mother y'all had gone to the store," Polly said. "Did you buy anything interesting?"

"Interesting? No," Mandie said, glancing at Joe. Snowball was sitting near her foot, and she quickly gave him a push. Snowball stood up and meowed loudly. "Oh, you want out, Snowball?" Mandie asked as she rose and started toward the door to the hall. "Come on. I'll let you out."

Snowball looked uncertainly at his mistress and then quickly followed her into the hallway. She opened the front door, but the cat didn't want to go out. He just stood there, looking up at his mistress. *Oh well*, she thought, *maybe that gave Polly enough time to change the subject*. Mandie didn't want Joe to know what she and Sallie had been doing that afternoon while the boys were at Polly's house. And she knew Polly was good at giving away secrets.

Mandie returned to the parlor and sat back down. Snowball ran off down the hallway toward the kitchen.

"I would love to see New Orleans sometime," Polly was saying to Joe.

"Then go see it," Jonathan spoke up, secretly grinning at Mandie.

Polly turned to look at Jonathan and said with a frown, "I plan to sometime soon, but I would like to visit New York first."

"Polly, we don't have all that many holidays from school," Mandie told her. "You may have to wait till summertime to do all this traveling you're planning."

"My mother can always get me out of school if

there's something we want to do," Polly replied.

"Then you'll never graduate from school to go to college if you take too much time off," Jonathan said.

Mandie heard the front door open again, and she quickly stepped to the doorway of the parlor to see who it was.

"It's just me," Dr. Woodard said as he came on down the corridor.

"I'm so glad you got back in time for supper," Mandie told him.

"I am, too, but I need to go and clean up," the doctor replied as he stopped to look inside the parlor. "Son, come with me. We need to talk a few minutes," he said to Joe.

"Yes, sir," Joe said, coming to join him in the hallway.

"We'll be back down in a few minutes," Dr. Woodard called back to Mandie as he and Joe went toward the staircase.

Mandie quickly rejoined her friends in the parlor. She decided the best thing to do was to explain to Polly about the party.

"Polly, we are planning on giving Joe a surprise going-away party on Monday night. You are welcome to help us, but please don't let Joe know what we are doing. That's what we went to the store for today," Mandie explained as she sat down near Polly. "We bought presents for him, and we're going to decorate the back parlor, but we'll have to do that after he goes to bed so he won't see us."

"I'll get him a present, too, and I want to help you decorate," Polly replied, her dark eyes sparkling with excitement. "I can run back home and ask my mother if I can spend the night with you."

"We have to make the decorations first," Sallie spoke up.

"Yes, and then we'll probably decorate tomorrow night," Mandie added.

"So I suppose I'd better buy a gift for Joe, too," Jonathan remarked as he listened to the conversation. "Will that store downtown be open on Monday?"

"It's open every day except Sunday," Mandie told him.

"I'll go with you, Jonathan, so I can buy something," Polly told him.

Jonathan looked at Mandie and shrugged his shoulders.

Mandie smiled at him and said, "Then I'll stay home and keep Joe occupied so he won't know what you are doing."

Polly looked at her thoughtfully with a frown. "Mandie, you could go with Jonathan, and I could stay here and keep Joe from finding out about things."

Mandie sighed loudly and said, "Polly, when do you plan to buy your present for Joe? I thought you wanted to go with Jonathan so you could purchase something."

"Well, I suppose I could go to the store as soon as they open Monday morning. It won't take me but a few minutes, and then I could come on over here and stay with Joe so Jonathan could go shopping," Polly explained. "And you could go with Jonathan, since he doesn't even know where the store is."

"No, Polly," Mandie objected. "I will stay here with Joe and you go with Jonathan. It will be much less complicated if we do it that way."

Jonathan looked at Polly and grinned as he said,

"What's the matter, Polly? Don't you want to go to the store with me?"

Polly became flustered and quickly replied, "Of course I do, Jonathan. I was just trying to arrange things more neatly. Of course I'll go with you. You just let me know what time Monday, and I will be ready."

"Then that's settled," Jonathan said, still smiling at Polly. "Secret matters tend to get complicated, don't they?" He looked at Mandie.

"They sure do," Mandie agreed.

Dr. Woodard returned to the parlor with Elizabeth, Mrs. Taft, and Joe. They all found seats around the room. Even Snowball strolled back in and went to stretch out on the warm hearth.

"It won't be long now till supper, just in case any of you young people are starving," Elizabeth remarked with a smile as she looked around the room.

"I'm absolutely weak with hunger," Jonathan said, grinning.

Mandie looked at Jonathan and said, "Aunt Lou knows how much you and Joe like to eat, so I'm sure she'll have plenty of everything." She glanced at Joe and noticed he was silent. She wondered what he and his father had discussed upstairs. "Oh well," she thought, "I can't know everything."

Aunt Lou came into the parlor to announce, "De food be on de table, Miz 'Liz'beth."

Elizabeth rose and said, "Thank you, Aunt Lou. We're on our way."

In the dining room the young people were at one end of the long table and the adults at the other. Mandie realized she wouldn't be able to hear a word of their conversation unless they spoke loudly, which they never did. But on the other hand, she and her friends could discuss their secrets without being overheard.

At the last minute Jason Bond came hurrying into the room.

"Sit with us, Mr. Jason," Mandie called to him.

The old man smiled and pulled out a chair across from Mandie. "I know what you're up to," he said with a big smile. "You think I might know something about your mysteries, right?"

"Well," Mandie said hesitantly. "Maybe you do. Have you learned anything about anything?" She passed him the bowl of potatoes that was sitting in front of her plate.

"Now, that covers a lot of territory," Mr. Bond said. "I did ask around the feedstore today if any of the real old-timers kept business journals on their farms back in the old days when there were quite a few large spreads around here. And guess what? They all did. In fact, they seemed to think I was asking a silly question. So there you have it. That old book must have been the Shaws' record for the farm." He put a potato on his plate and reached for the platter of ham.

"It looks so old. It must have been a long time ago," Mandie replied. "But, anyway, I'll still ask Uncle John about it whenever he comes back home."

"You didn't find any trace of that turkey, did you?" Jonathan asked. He grinned at the old man.

"No, I wasn't really looking for that bird because it must be long gone by now, nevermore to be seen by us," Jason Bond replied. He continued filling his plate as the young people passed the food.

"Maybe when Uncle John comes back home he

can help us out," Mandie said. "He may know something about the quilt, too, Sallie." She looked at her Cherokee friend.

"Yes, he is part Cherokee, and his white people gave a home to the Cherokee people for a long time," Sallie said. "Remember, Mandie, that my grandfather lived here also at one time."

"That's right. Uncle Ned told me about that," Mandie agreed as she buttered a hot biscuit.

Aunt Lou was standing at the sideboard ready to wait on the table. Liza came in through the doorway from the hall. Mandie glanced her way.

"I needs to give a message to de doctuh," Liza said, looking at the old woman.

"A message? Whut kinda message?" Aunt Lou asked.

"De man he say important message," Liza replied. "De man at de do' he say his friend got hurt bad, need de doctuh," Liza explained.

Everyone at the table had stopped to listen.

"A man is hurt, Liza?" Dr. Woodard asked.

"Yes, suh," Liza replied. "He wait at de do' to take you to de hurt man."

Dr. Woodard stood up, laid down his napkin, and said, "I'd better go see what this is all about."

"You really should finish your supper, Dr. Woodard. You've been making calls all day," Elizabeth said.

"I'll be right back and finish what's on my plate," the old doctor told her as he left the room.

"An accident? The man must have had an accident of some kind, don't you think?" Mandie asked her friends.

"Yes," Sallie agreed.

"I know my father has to go whenever he's

needed, but I know he's tired, too," Joe remarked. "He has been all the way across the mountain today making calls."

"Maybe it won't take long, whatever needs to be done," Mandie said.

Dr. Woodard came back in a couple of minutes and sat down at the table. "Seems the man fell somewhere over near the mountain," he said. "I told the man to wait while I finish my supper."

"Liza, you go git Abraham hitch up de doctuh's horse and buggy so's he don't hafta do dat," Aunt Lou told the young girl.

"Yessum, I do dat," Liza said and left the room.

Dr. Woodard was finished eating in a few minutes, and everyone else was done, as well. They all rose to follow the doctor out of the room.

"I'll run up and get your bag," Joe told his father and ran up the stairs.

The adults went to sit in the parlor, while the doctor waited at the parlor doorway for Joe to bring his bag. The young people stood around and then followed the doctor to the front door when he was ready to leave.

"I may be late," Dr. Woodard called back. "The man is way over on the mountain."

Mandie looked outside. There was a man standing beside a horse down at the gate to the road. Although the daylight was failing, she thought he looked familiar.

"That man," she said to her friends. "Have y'all ever seen him before?"

The young people watched as Dr. Woodard hurried out to the driveway where Abraham had his buggy waiting. He jumped in and drove on down to the gate. The stranger got on his horse and led the way down the road.

"I don't believe I've ever seen him, but then I don't know everybody here because I don't live here," Joe remarked.

"I sure don't recognize him," Jonathan added.

Mandie looked at Sallie and together they said, "That man in the store."

Joe asked, "That man in the store? What does that mean?"

"I think Sallie and I saw him in the store—one day," Mandie said, fearing Joe would ask when they were in the store.

"Anyhow, I hope my father is not gone long," Joe remarked.

The girls walked ahead of the boys back to the front porch and inside.

"It's cold out there," Joe remarked as he and Jonathan went into the parlor, where the fire warmed the room.

Mandie pulled at Sallie's hand at the doorway of the parlor and whispered, "I'm sure that was the man who bumped into me at the store today."

"Yes, I think he was," Sallie agreed.

"And I don't believe he lives here," Mandie said.

"Dr. Woodard may be able to tell us something when he returns," Sallie suggested.

"He was a strange-acting man," Mandie declared. "I'll be anxious to find out where Dr. Woodard went and who the injured man is. Maybe he is someone who lives here in Franklin."

The girls entered the parlor and sat down. Mandie's mind was still trying to figure out this latest mystery.

Chapter 8 / One Missing

Mandie and Sallie were up early the next morning. As soon as they were dressed, they went down to the kitchen to find out who was coming to breakfast. Snowball followed them.

"I dun had Liza lay out de food fo' y'all in de dinin' room 'cause Miz 'Liz'beth say last night she and yo' grandma gonna sleep late, what wid de men all bein' gone," Aunt Lou told Mandie. She was sitting at her table in the kitchen drinking coffee. She rose to set a plate of scraps down by the stove for the cat.

"I was hoping we could eat with you in here where it's nice and warm," Mandie said with a disappointed smile.

"It ain't cold in de dinin' room. Abraham dun made dat fire over an hour ago," Aunt Lou replied.

"Have Joe and Jonathan been for their breakfast yet?" Mandie asked.

"Ain't seed 'em yit," the old woman told her.

"Now you jes' git on in de dinin' room. Liza waitin' fo' y'all in dere, my chile." She sat back down.

"All right, if we have to," Mandie said with a smile, turning back toward the door. "Come on, Sallie. Let's go eat everything up before the boys get it."

"That would be hard to do," Sallie said, following her out of the room.

When the girls entered the dining room, Liza was putting white linen napkins and silverware on the matching white linen tablecloth covering the long dining table. She looked up at the girls and said, "Ev'rything dun ready over dere." She pointed to the sideboard laden with covered dishes.

Mandie crossed the room to pick up a plate from the sideboard. Sallie followed. "Have Joe and Jonathan been in to eat yet?" she asked, raising a silver lid on a dish to get a hot biscuit.

"I ain't seed 'em," Liza said, finishing laying the silverware and napkins. She straightened up and looked at Mandie. "Only one been in to eat was Mistuh Bond. He dun et and run off somewhere on bidness he say."

"He's always going somewhere on business for Uncle John," Mandie said, filling her plate with grits, bacon, and eggs.

Sallie put two hot biscuits on her plate, covered them with black molasses, and added a piece of ham on the side.

When the girls sat down at the table with their food, Liza brought the coffeepot and filled their cups. "You reckon dat doctuh son dun run off to dat cullege place he be talkin' 'bout?" Liza asked, taking the coffeepot back to the sideboard and placing it on the rack over the warming flame.

Mandie laughed and said, "No, I don't think he'd be gone to college. He's probably not up yet, or Jonathan, either." She sipped her coffee.

"It is early for us to be up," Sallie reminded her, slicing the ham on her plate.

The door suddenly opened, and Joe and Jonathan rushed into the room.

"Well, so y'all are up and—" Mandie began.

"My father didn't come back last night," Joe interrupted her as he walked over to the sideboard, picked up a cup and saucer, and poured coffee. Jonathan did likewise.

Mandie was alarmed. "Dr. Woodard didn't come back last night?" she asked, dropping her fork onto her plate and quickly swallowing the mouthful of food. She looked at Joe. He seemed awfully worried. Quickly pushing back her chair, she stood up. "Come sit by me and eat something, Joe, while we discuss this," she told him. She pulled out the chair next to her.

Joe, with both hands on the cup and saucer, walked over to the table and sat down next to Mandie. "I'm not really hungry," he protested. "I can't think about anything but what happened to my father."

Jonathan filled his plate at the sideboard and sat down by Sallie. "You need to eat something," he told Joe.

Liza quickly picked up a plate on the sideboard and began loading it with food from the various dishes. She brought it over to the table, placed it in front of Joe, and said, "I'se gwine act like Aunt Lou now. You'se gwine eat all dat food and no fuss 'bout it." She stood by his chair.

Joe looked up at her and said, between a frown

and a slight smile, "You can't act like Aunt Lou, Liza. You're not big enough."

"I mought not be big 'nuff, but I sho' knows how to go git Aunt Lou, and she make you eat," Liza told him and went back to watch from the sideboard.

"Liza, I think you ought to go get Aunt Lou anyway," Mandie told the girl. "We need to ask her if she knows anything about Dr. Woodard."

"Sho' nuff," Liza said and hurried out the door.

"Joe, your father did say he might be late, so maybe the man was seriously ill and he had to stay awhile. He also said it was a long way off, so all that would take time," Mandie told Joe.

Joe finally sipped his coffee and said, "I know. I've considered all that. But it's after seven o'clock in the morning, and he's been gone since right after supper last night."

"I suppose you looked to see if his horse and buggy were in the barn?" Mandie asked.

Joe nodded and said, "They're not there."

"We also looked around the neighborhood to see if he might have had trouble with the horse or the buggy and got stranded somewhere, but nobody has seen him," Jonathan said, slowly beginning to eat his food.

"Perhaps my grandfather will return this morning and he will find your father, Joe," Sallie said.

Joe smiled at the Cherokee girl and said, "Thanks, Sallie. I know if anyone could find my father, Uncle Ned could."

"This would happen with all the men gone," Mandie said with a sigh. Then she quickly looked at Joe, who was pushing the food around on his plate with a fork. "Joe, we'll just have to take charge. The four of us will have to search the whole town and all the roads going out.''

Aunt Lou had come into the room while Mandie was speaking, followed by Liza. ''Now, whut is dis 'bout de doctuh not comin' back?'' she asked as she came to stand by the table. Liza went back to the sideboard.

Joe explained that his father had not returned. The old woman listened and frowned as he spoke. ''I'm afraid something has happened,'' Joe ended.

''Now, don't you worry 'bout your papa,'' Aunt Lou told him. ''De sick man musta bin terrible sick. Why, de doctuh prob'ly gwine come down dat drive-way any minute now.''

''Aunt Lou,'' Mandie said, ''I think we ought to go out and look for him, the four of us, that is.'' She motioned to include her friend. ''If Mother and Grandmother are not downstairs by the time we finish breakfast, we could go on, and you could explain to them where we went.''

''But, my chile, how I knows where y'all go? And how y'all gwine know if de doctuh come back and y'all out somewheres lookin' fo' him?'' the old woman asked.

''The four of us can split up,'' Mandie said, quickly swallowing a bit of bacon. ''Jonathan and Sallie can look all around the town, and Joe and I can go out on the roads. There will be lots of people out on the country roads because today is Sunday and they'll be going to church. We can ask everyone we see to let Dr. Woodard know where we are if they see him.''

Aunt Lou thought for a moment. ''I s'pose dat wouldn't do no harm,'' she finally concluded. ''But mind you, my chile. Don't you and Joe be gone too long. Else somebody hafta come look fo' y'all."

Mandie looked around the table at her friends. "Is this agreeable with y'all?" she asked.

Everyone nodded their approval.

"Now, don't y'all be goin' off too long," Aunt Lou warned them. "Miz 'Liz'beth and Miz Taft dey be down befo' long."

"We won't, Aunt Lou," Mandie promised as the old woman left the dining room.

The four hurried through their breakfast, put on their coats and hats, and were soon outside to begin their search. Snowball followed his mistress.

"Joe and I will begin on the main road out of town," Mandie told Sallie. "You know your way around in Franklin, so you and Jonathan go up and down every street and every alley and look in everybody's yard."

"We will do that, Mandie," Sallie agreed as Jonathan nodded.

"What exactly are we supposed to do if we locate Dr. Woodard?" Jonathan asked.

"Just tell him to go back to Mandie's house and you, too, and wait for us," Joe said.

When the four got to the gate at the road, they separated. Sallie and Jonathan began walking toward the center of town. Mandie and Joe went in the opposite direction, which led them out into the countryside. Still unnoticed by his mistress, Snowball bounced along behind them until they stopped.

Mandie slowed down to look up a trail leading off the road to the right. "Do you think we ought to go up there?" she asked Joe.

Both of them stopped to look.

"I don't think my father could have gone up that

path. It's not wide enough for his buggy to get through," Joe told her.

"You're right," Mandie agreed. "It probably goes to one house."

Joe said, "There sure aren't many people out this morning. I suppose when it gets time to go to church, everyone will be on the road."

Mandie shivered slightly as she pulled her coat collar tighter around her neck. "It's just too cold to be out unless you have a definite purpose," she said, then added, "Like we do, and your father."

Snowball began swishing by Mandie's legs. She bent down to pick him up. "I figured you would be right behind us," she told the cat as she held him in her arms. "Your feet are ice cold." She rubbed his paws.

Joe smiled and said, "If you carry him, you will both be warmer."

"He's so heavy I can't hurry, but I suppose I'll have to tote him," Mandie replied.

They walked on for almost two miles before they saw anyone outside, and then it turned out to be an old woman. As they approached a falling-down log house on the road, a dog began barking ferociously. Snowball growled and dug his sharp claws into the shoulder of Mandie's coat.

"Oh no!" Mandie quickly stopped in the road as she tried to see where the dog was.

"Stand there a minute," Joe told her as the animal continued barking. He stepped ahead, and Mandie watched as a large brown mixed-breed dog appeared out of the bushes in the front yard of the shack. Joe looked back at Mandie and said, "He's on a rope. We can get on by all right. He can't reach us."

Mandie slowly moved forward to join Joe as she held firmly to her white cat. "Let's hurry and get past him," she told Joe.

The two began moving faster, and the dog began barking louder. Just as they came in front of the house, an old woman came out of the undergrowth with a shotgun aimed directly at them.

"We're only passing by," Joe called to her over the noise of the dog.

"Don't move another step, you hear?" the woman yelled at them as she walked closer.

"We're sorry for disturbing your dog, but we are not coming into your yard," Mandie said in a loud voice.

The woman came closer with the shotgun still pointed at the two, and then suddenly she dropped the gun down to her side as she laughed wildly and cried out, "Well, if it ain't the doctor's son!"

"You know my father?" Joe quickly asked as the three of them stood there with the dog still making a loud protest.

The woman turned back for a second toward the animal and yelled, "Now, cut that racket out, Mud, you hear. Shut up right now. Be quiet!"

Mandie and Joe watched as the dog obeyed and sat down in the bushes to watch them.

"Now, what is the doctor's son doing out here on this lonely road so early in the morning, and Sunday morning at that?" the woman asked.

Mandie looked her over as Snowball finally settled down in her arms. The woman was toothless, had thin gray hair, and was wearing only a thin shawl around the shoulders of her faded cotton dress. She must be very poor.

"We are looking for my father, ma'am," Joe replied. "Have you by any chance seen him?"

"Have I seen your doctor father?" the woman repeated. "Of course, I saw your father when he drove past here last night. Old Mud here saw him, too, and started that yelping he does when he sees a friend, so I looked out the window and saw Dr. Woodard coming down the road in his buggy. I thought perhaps he was coming to check on my rheumatism, but he didn't even slow up, kept going, and so I thought, there must be someone mighty sick because he sure was in a hurry."

"We're staying at the Shaws' house. This is Mandie Shaw. And my father went out on a call after supper last night and has not come back yet," Joe explained.

"Yes, I know who the Shaws are. Mighty good family, they are," the woman said. "Been knowing those people all my life, I reckon. Now, I wonder where the doctor went. Not many houses beyond here before you get into the mountain, you know."

"He might have gone on into the mountain," Mandie said.

"But there's no one living in the mountain but bootleggers and beggars," the woman said. "But then again, I suppose one of those bootleggers might have fallen ill and had to have a doctor."

"But the man who came to our house to get Dr. Woodard said he had a friend who had been injured," Mandie told her.

"Well, come to think of it, I suppose some of those bootleggers could have been shooting each other, or they could have shot a beggar. I wouldn't worry about it too much if I were y'all. I'm sure they are not going to shoot the doctor," the woman said.

Mandie took a deep breath as she looked up at

Joe, who was frowning. She turned back to the woman and asked, "I'm sorry, but I don't believe we got your name, ma'am."

The woman grinned at her and said, "Not many people nowadays that want to know my name, but since you told me yours, I reckon I ought to tell you mine. People call me Miz Maude Metts, but I've always said that's not right because I have never been married and they ought to call me Miss Maude Metts." She laughed.

Joe held out his hand and said, "I'm glad to meet you, Miss Maude Metts."

The woman shook his hand and said, "I knew the doctor's son would do things right because his father does. He's the only one who calls me by the right name, bless his heart."

"Thank you, Miss Metts," Joe said with a smile, and turning to look down the road, he said, "I suppose we'd better go on. If we don't hurry and get this done and get back to Mandie's house, I'm afraid her mother will be upset with us."

"I don't think her mother will be, but now that grandmother of hers, that's a different story," Miss Metts replied.

Mandie grinned at her and said, "I know exactly what you mean."

"Do you live here alone?" Joe asked as they started forward. He paused.

"Sure do, always have, just me and Mud, and he's getting on in age now," the woman said. "Don't know what I'll do if he passes on to dog heaven one of these days. Won't have no bodyguard."

"Don't you worry about that, Miss Metts. We'll get you another watchdog if that happens," Mandie told her.

Joe quickly said, "I was just thinking. My dog, Samantha, had several puppies a while back, and they're old enough now that you could train one of them to be your watchdog. Would you like my father to bring you one next time he comes to see you, Miss Metts?"

"Oh, you don't mean that!" the old woman exclaimed with a big toothless grin. "You mean I could really have one of those puppies?"

"Why, sure," Joe said, smiling back. "Only thing, you'd have to train Mud there not to hurt the puppy until they get acquainted with each other."

"Don't worry about Mud. I would keep the puppy in the house if your father brings me one," Miss Metts said, still smiling. "Now, wouldn't that be something? A brand-new addition to my family. That would make three of us."

"Yes, ma'am," Joe said and started to walk on again. "As soon as I find my father, I'll tell him you want one of the puppies. If you happen to see my father, Miss Metts, I'd appreciate it if you would tell him everyone at Mandie's house is wondering where he is."

"I certainly will, and I certainly thank you ahead of time for the puppy," Miss Metts said, then humming to herself, she turned and disappeared through the bushes in front of the house.

As Joe and Mandie continued down the road, Mandie said, "That was an interesting woman, wasn't she?"

Joe looked down at her and replied, "She sure is. I've heard my father speak of her. At one time she came from a wealthy family. Come to think of it, she has a college education, Mandie, and that's unusual for a country woman like that."

Mandie grinned mischievously as she looked up at him and said, "Why, Joe Woodard, that's not unusual for a country woman to have a college education. You are looking at a future one right now."

"I know," Joe said, grinning back. "What I meant was that it's unusual to find a woman living in poverty like that with a college education."

"Does your father think she's all here, you know what I mean? Is she slightly off somehow?" Mandie asked.

"Mandie Shaw! What a silly question!" Joe teased her. "What made you think such a thing? That is a woman ahead of her time, with a mind of her own."

"If you say so," Mandie replied, still holding Snowball tightly. "Joe, do you remember she said there were only bootleggers and beggars living in the mountain? I hope we don't run into any of them."

"I know," Joe said with a sigh. "I should have brought my rifle, but I didn't even think about it. We forgot to ask Miss Metts if there was a man with my father, you know, the man who came to your house to get him."

"She didn't mention anyone else, so I would think she didn't see him," Mandie answered as they hurried on. "So maybe the stranger didn't go all the way to where the sick man was. Maybe he just told your father how to get there, and Dr. Woodard went on alone."

"Could be," Joe agreed. "But if the injured man was the stranger's friend, you'd think he would be going back to see what the doctor had to say about him."

"This whole thing sounds all mixed up to me,"

Mandie said. "I'm pretty sure the man who came to our house was the same man Sallie and I saw in the store."

"You mentioned that before," Joe said, looking down at her. "Just when did you see this man? When were you in the store where you saw him?"

Mandie looked back up at him and decided it was time to explain about the store. She would have to give away her secret, but it might help in locating Dr. Woodard. She took a long breath and said, "Joe Woodard, I never can keep a secret from you." She grinned.

Joe gave her a puzzled smile and said, "That's right, so you might as well tell all."

"Well, it's like this," Mandie began. "Sallie and I went to the store yesterday afternoon while you and Jonathan were over at Polly's house." She paused.

"And?" Joe asked.

"And we went to the store to do some shopping." Mandie tried evading the real reason. "We thought it might be fun to give you a going-away present or something."

"Oh, Mandie, I'm sorry. I shouldn't have insisted. Now I've ruined your surprise," Joe apologized.

"Not all of it. And you can just pretend to be surprised when we give you the presents," Mandie told him. "Anyhow, this man in the store bumped into me, and I apologized, but he didn't say a word. He just kept walking right on through the store. I thought he acted awfully strange. Sallie did, too."

"And you believe that's the same man who came to your house after my father?" Joe questioned. "You know what I'm thinking? That man may be an outlaw of some kind. I hope my father is safe."

"Joe, I'm sorry," Mandie said, suddenly stopping in the middle of the road. "Joe, we need to say our verse." She reached for his hand as he, too, paused there.

Holding hands, the two recited Mandie's favorite verse, " 'What time I am afraid I will put my trust in Thee.' "

Mandie looked up at Joe and smiled. "Now I feel better. Your father is going to be all right."

"Yes, I think so," Joe agreed and gave her a quick squeeze around the shoulders and then started on down the road.

Mandie hurried along at his side, wondering what they would find ahead, but not as worried as she had been. Everything would work out just fine, she was sure.

Chapter 9 / Danger!

As Mandie and Joe walked along the road, they began to meet a few people, most of whom, judging from the clothes they were wearing, were headed into town to church services. And there were several people going in their direction. The two young people tried flagging down the vehicles traveling toward Franklin, but most of the occupants either thought they were just waving at them or didn't seem to notice them.

Finally an old wagon, with half its top cover missing, carrying an old man, a young woman, and six children, slowed down as it met up with Mandie and Joe.

"Hello!" Mandie began yelling and waving for them to stop.

Joe started making signs, too, as he stepped toward the middle of the road when the wagon rolled to a stop. He looked up at the man and asked,

"Sir, have you seen Dr. Woodard back down the road you just came up?"

Mandie came to his side and quickly added, "We're trying to find Dr. Woodard."

"You're trying to find a doctor? Is someone sick?" the old man asked, squinting and leaning forward to look at them.

Before Mandie or Joe could reply, the young woman quickly spoke, "No, Papa, don't you recognize this young fellow? He's Dr. Woodard's son. I've seen him with his father several times when the doctor came to see Mama. He always stayed outside."

"Is this so?" the old man asked, leaning closer to look at Joe. "In that case, I must ask what you are doing walking way out here in the country looking for the doctor?"

"I remember you, Mr. Harrison," Joe told the man. "And I remember Mrs. Harrison."

"May her soul rest in peace," Mr. Harrison murmured in a sad voice. "Now, you didn't answer my question. What are you doing walking out here in the country looking for your father?"

"My father left the Shaws' house last night after supper to go see a man who was injured somewhere near the mountain. A stranger came to the Shaws to ask him to go, and my father has not returned."

"I'm Mandie Shaw," Mandie explained. "I think I saw the stranger in Stovall's store yesterday. I don't believe he is from around here."

"Oh dear!" the young woman exclaimed. "Did Dr. Woodard not tell you exactly where he was going? He didn't give you anyone's name?" She looked from Mandie to Joe.

The six children in the back of the wagon had all

been quiet and seemed to be listening to the conversation. Now the oldest boy, about twelve years old, pulled on the woman's sleeve. "Mama," he said so low that Mandie could barely understand what he was saying, "Henry Stone told me this morning when I saw him in his yard that his father saw Dr. Woodard go past our houses last night and that his father was wondering if someone was sick."

"He did?" Mandie quickly said.

"Julius, are you sure?" the woman asked, and turning to the two young people, she explained, "The Stones live across the road from us."

"Yes, ma'am, I'm sure that Henry told me that," the boy replied.

"Do you remember whether your friend Henry said my father was alone or not?" Joe asked, stepping closer to the side of the wagon where the boy was sitting.

Julius thought for a moment and then said, "I don't believe he said whether Dr. Woodard was alone or not."

"Why don't we go on and stop and talk to Mr. Stone?" she asked Joe.

"Mr. Stone left before I saw Henry this morning," Julius explained. "Henry said his father would be gone on a hunting trip for two or three days."

Mr. Harrison leaned back to ask the boy, "Do you know where he went to hunt?"

"No, sir, Henry didn't say," Julius replied.

Mr. Harrison turned back to Joe and said, "I would advise you to go on and talk to Mrs. Stone. She may know something. I'm sorry about your problem, but if we don't go on, we'll be late for church." He tightened his hold on the reins, which he had let slack off.

"If there's anything we can do, you just let us know, you hear?" the woman called to them as Mr. Harrison drove the wagon on toward town.

"Thank you," Joe and Mandie both called to her.

"I suppose you know where the Harrisons live in order for us to find the Stones, who live across the road from them?" Mandie asked.

"It has been a long time, maybe four or five years," Joe replied, "but I know they live on this road. We'll just keep going until I see a house that I recognize as theirs."

"At least someone saw your father, but we still don't know whether that stranger was with him or not," Mandie said.

The two hurried on down the road. With the weight of Snowball on her shoulder, Mandie had trouble keeping up with Joe's long strides, but she didn't complain. She knew Joe was worried about his father. They walked for what seemed like several miles to Mandie before they even saw a house of any kind.

"I see a building up ahead on the left side," Mandie said, pointing up the road and squinting to see.

Joe stopped and held his hand over his brow to shade his eyes as he, too, gazed in that direction. "That may be a barn," he said.

"If there's a barn up there, wouldn't there be a house somewhere nearby?" Mandie asked.

"Most likely," Joe agreed. "We'll soon find out."

The two hurried on and were soon near enough to see that the building was a barn. And farther back from the road were the remains of a house that had burned to the ground a while ago and was now sprouting weeds between the burnt timbers.

"Oh, I wonder what happened to the people who lived there?" Mandie asked, catching her breath as they stood on the road looking at it. "It looks so sad."

"Yes, it does," Joe agreed. "I don't remember anything about that house. My father never visited it when I was with him that I can remember. And there's nothing across the road, so there's no one to ask about it. Let's move on."

They finally sighted another house in the distance, and as they approached it, Mandie saw another house across the road from it.

"The Harrisons must live in one house and the Stones in the other," Mandie remarked as they came closer. The houses were similarly made of hand-hewn logs and with enormous rock chimneys running up the end of each one.

"Yes, the Harrisons live on the left and the Stones on the right," Joe confirmed. "I remember the place now." He stopped in front of the Harrisons' house to look. "I remember they had lots of chickens running all over the yard and the road. While I waited in the buggy when my father went inside to doctor Mrs. Harrison, I wondered if any of the chickens ever got run over. They had a dog tied up over at the end of the porch there." He pointed to the right.

"I don't see any chickens or a dog now," Mandie remarked.

"No, neither do I, but let's go over here and see if the Stones are home," Joe replied, walking over to the pathway that led to the Stones' house.

Mandie quickly caught up with him, holding tightly to Snowball. "I hope they don't have a dog anywhere near," she said.

At that moment a ferocious bark came from somewhere behind the house. Snowball dug his claws into the shoulder of Mandie's coat, and Mandie stopped to look around.

"He's tied in the back. I can see him," Joe told her as he went ahead toward the front door.

Mandie followed, and when she reached the end of the porch, she could see a huge black dog straining against the rope that had him tied to a small tree trunk. She quickly went up the steps behind Joe.

Joe knocked on the front door. Mandie tried to soothe Snowball as the dog continued barking. There was no answer, and finally Joe turned back to her.

"There must not be anyone home," he said in a disappointed voice.

"Julius said Mr. Stone left on a hunting trip, remember?" Mandie reminded him. "So Mrs. Stone and the others are most likely gone to church."

"Probably," Joe agreed. He started back down the front steps. "Well, I suppose we can just keep on walking because we know my father did come this far and went on past, according to Julius."

Mandie caught up with him, and they walked back to the road. "Maybe there'll be someone home at the next house," she said.

But the next house was a long way off, and when they finally got to it, they found it deserted, too. On the left side of the road, which had become narrower, was an old wooden shack that had its roof falling in, its window lights gone, and the porch across the entire front leaning lopsided with one of the support posts dangling in the air. Weeds and underbrush covered most of the yard, but the walkway to the back of the house seemed to have been cleared off recently.

The two young people stood and stared at the house from the road. "Well, shall we look inside?" Mandie asked, looking up at Joe.

"Inside?" Joe exclaimed. "There is nothing inside that house, I'm sure. I imagine the floors inside are even gone."

"We could go look through a window," Mandie suggested as Snowball squirmed on her shoulder, wanting down. She started forward and then waited for Joe to join her. "Are you coming?"

"Oh, Mandie, I'll go with you, but you can see there's nothing left of this house," Joe protested as he walked along with her to a window opening on the side.

"Look!" Mandie exclaimed, sticking her head through the opening and pointing inside. "Someone has been here. And the floor in this room at least is not caved in." There was a stack of quilts in a far corner.

"Evidently someone has been camping out here," Joe agreed as he, too, looked through the window. He straightened up and stepped back. "Mandie, they could be outlaws for all we know. We shouldn't go poking around here. It might be dangerous if someone saw us."

Mandie turned to walk over to the pathway toward the back. "They've been using this trail through the bushes. Let's go see where it goes," she told Joe.

"Mandie, we really ought to get going if we're to find my father."

Mandie quickly walked down the pathway that had been cleared recently and found it took her directly to the back door and then seemed to branch off into the thick bushes at the back of the yard. The back porch was in better shape than the front porch, and she went up the three steps onto it and hurried to the back door that was shut. She tried the doorknob and was surprised when it turned easily and the door swung open without the slightest creak.

"Joe, come on," she said as she stepped through the doorway.

"Mandie," Joe protested but followed her.

They were in what had evidently been the kitchen. There was a crude table and two cracker barrels pulled up to it for chairs. Tin plates and eating utensils were on the table. A bucket of water stood on a shelf in a corner. On another shelf at the far side was food in bags and jars.

"Hmmm!" Joe murmured as he looked around. "Someone is definitely staying here, and I think we'd better get out before they come back." He looked at Mandie.

"Look, Joe, they've even rigged up an old quilt on the wall that can be let down over the window," she said, walking over to the huge rock fireplace. "And they have wood in a pile here in the corner to make a fire."

"Mandie! Let's go!" Joe said in a firm voice.

"Wait till I look in the other rooms," Mandie said, opening a door and finding herself in the front room they had looked at through the broken window. She quickly looked around. There was no other door. The house had only two rooms.

"Mandie, let's go," Joe said from the doorway to the room.

"I'm coming," Mandie replied. She tripped on an uneven floorboard as she turned, and Snowball managed to escape from her arms.

Joe reached out a hand to keep her from falling. "You see, this place is absolutely falling in and is dangerous."

Mandie quickly looked around for her white cat. He had run across the kitchen and was pawing at a quilt wadded up in the far corner. "Come on, Snowball," she said, hurrying to capture the cat before he could get away. "Let's go." As she bent down to pick him up, his claws hung in the old quilt and dragged it along with him. Mandie pulled at the bedcovering and was about to throw it down when she glimpsed something in the corner where it had been lying. "Joe! There's something here!" she exclaimed, holding on to the cat and kneeling to look in the dark corner.

Joe joined her, and he reached forward to pull whatever it was into the light from the window. "Mandie, I do believe this is a bag of ammunition," he said, opening the dirty bag. "It is! We'd better get out of here fast. Outlaws are probably holed up in this house, and there's no telling what they would do to us if they found us in here." He pulled closed the bag, put it back where it had been, and covered it with the quilt.

"Oh, Joe, too late! I hear someone walking outside," Mandie said in a loud whisper. "Where can we hide?" She gazed around the room and then slipped back into the front room. Joe silently followed. The two crept back into a dark corner and tried to be quiet. Mandie leaned up against something bumpy behind her and felt around in the dim area to see what it was. "Joe, there's a ladder to the loft here! Come on!" she told him as she turned and quickly began her way up, holding on to Snowball with one arm.

There was a light footstep on the back porch, and Joe immediately scrambled up the ladder behind her.

The loft was dark except for a little light filtering through the holes in the roof. Mandie could see that it was roughly floored, and she moved silently to one side, stooped down, and held Snowball tightly, hoping and praying he would not make a sound.

Joe softly stepped over to join her and sat on the floor.

Mandie bit her bottom lip to keep it from trembling in fear as she tried to see around the dark attic. It was empty. There was not one piece of anything up there that she could see. Therefore, whoever was downstairs would not have a reason to come upstairs, she hoped.

The man downstairs was moving quietly around the room. Mandie heard a faint tinkle that sounded as though the man was moving the tin dishes slightly, and he seemed to be talking to himself, "Oh, where is it?" Then a clatter of a tin plate, or something metal, being dropped, and the man said, "Ah, there it is. I knew I'd find it."

The two upstairs heard the man close the back door with a loud slam. Mandie scrambled to the opening in the eaves to try to see down in the yard and found the roof of the back porch was outside where they were. She squeezed through the broken boards and managed to step out onto the roof.

"Mandie, what are you doing?" Joe exclaimed softly as he watched.

"Joe, look, the man's down there!" she exclaimed, looking back at Joe. "And he is the man who came to my house for your father. Quick, Joe, come look!''

Joe hastily pushed through the opening, snagging his coat without noticing it, and looked down into the yard. The stranger was walking toward the bushes at the back, and the two saw him lead out a horse that he was preparing to mount.

"Mandie, are you sure that's the man who came to your house?" Joe whispered.

"Yes, I can even see the black patch on the knee of his trousers! He's the same man we saw in the store!" Mandie exclaimed. "Oh, Joe, he's going to get away!"

The man threw the reins onto a limb nearby and walked back into the underbrush. Mandie and Joe watched, but he had disappeared from sight.

"Where did he go?" Mandie said, mostly to herself, as she clutched Snowball.

The two were practically lying on the roof in order not to be seen, and they listened for the man to return. There was not a sound. Minutes passed, and Mandie was beginning to think the man had just decided to go off somewhere and leave the horse standing there in the yard.

Suddenly the man came back out of the bushes, carrying what looked like a heavy bag this time. He walked over to the horse and fastened the bag onto the saddle, then stepped into the saddle.

Mandie noticed that Joe was sliding his way closer to the edge of the tin roof. She tried to follow him but was afraid Snowball would manage to get loose. "Joe! Don't get too close! You could fall off!" she cautioned.

Joe looked back at her and whispered, "You are

sure this is the same man who came to your house after my father?"

"Yes, he is. I'm positive he is," Mandie confirmed.

Mandie gasped in horror as Joe suddenly stood up on the very edge of the roof, and when the stranger began moving slowly forward on the horse toward the front of the house, Joe made a diving leap off the porch and landed squarely on top of the stranger on the horse. "Joe!" she screamed.

The man was taken by surprise, and Joe managed to knock him off the horse. Mandie watched, her heart beating so fast she was dizzy, as the two wrestled on the ground and the horse wandered into the bushes.

"Oh, Joe! That man's twice as big as you! You can't beat him up!" Mandie cried, her face flooded with tears.

Snowball was loudly protesting her hold on him, and when she reached to wipe her eyes, he managed to wiggle loose. He ran over to the edge of the roof, looked down, and then sailed off the roof and landed on the back of the stranger below.

"Oh, Snowball, he'll kill you!" Mandie cried, watching as the white cat sank sharp claws into the man's back, causing him to howl in pain and giving Joe an opportunity to break his grasp.

Mandie, trembling in fright, looked up at the heavens and said, "Oh, dear God, please help us! 'What time I am afraid I will put my trust in Thee.'"

She felt the strength come to her to get to her feet. She raced back across the roof toward the opening to get into the attic and from there to get down to the backyard.

"Joe, I'm coming!" she called as she ran through the house.

Chapter 10 / Strangers

When Mandie got down to the kitchen, she could see through the open window into the backyard. She came to a screeching halt as she slipped on the uneven floorboards in the kitchen. Realizing the man probably didn't know anyone else was around, she tried to figure out how she could help Joe.

"The bag of ammunition! It's heavy, but I think I can carry it," she declared to herself as she hastily pulled the bag out of its hiding place in the corner. A heavy rope made a drawstring for the bag, and she used that as a handle. The bag felt as though it weighed almost half as much as she did, but she figured she would be able to swing it by the rope.

"And the best way to surprise that man would be to go out the front and come around to the backyard," she said to herself. She hurried to the front door, straining under the weight of the bag, managed to push the warped thing open, and stepped outside onto the shaky porch. Staying up against the front of the house, just in case the porch fell in, she dragged the bag behind her and then stepped off the end of the porch, straight into a thicket of briars.

"Oh, shucks!" she exclaimed as she worked to get her coat free. She was under such a strain she didn't even feel the prick of the many sharp points on her legs or on her hands as she pulled them away.

"Now!" she exclaimed to herself as she gave a mighty tug against the briars and stepped into the cleared part of the yard. Wrapping the rope around one wrist, she lifted the heavy bag and slowly made her way to the back of the house.

"Oh no!" she exclaimed under her breath as she peeked around the corner. The stranger had one of Joe's arms pulled behind him, and Joe was in great pain.

"I'm asking you again. Where is my father?" Joe gasped for breath as he tried to get free.

"I ain't seen no doctor. You tell me whut you doin' ramblin' round here, if you know whut's good fer you," the man ordered, giving Joe's arm a sharp tug.

Joe winced in pain but did not cry out.

Mandie did cry out in pain as she rushed forward, swung the bag into the air, and clobbered the man in the back of the head. The stranger sank to the ground and did not move.

"Oh, Joe!" she cried and rushed to his side where he had sat down on the ground when the man released his hold. He was rubbing his arm and shaking his head.

"Mandie! You conked him out," Joe managed to say with pain in his voice.

Mandie began rubbing Joe's hand, glanced at the man on the ground, and asked, "Did I kill him?"

"Mandie, I hope not!" Joe exclaimed. He rotated his arm and added, "I'll be all right soon as the circulation gets going again."

The man on the ground groaned. Joe quickly slid over to him and pulled his pistol from his belt.

Mandie watched and said, "Joe, let's pull the rope out of that bag of ammunition and use it to tie him up." She ran to drag the bag over near them.

"I'll have to cut the rope in two to get it out," Joe said, looking around for something to use.

Mandie gazed around the yard, trying to figure out how she could get the string out of the bag. She saw Snowball over near the porch scratching in the weeds. "Snowball, come here! We don't want to have to chase you down," she called to him as she ran to pick him up. Glancing down at the weeds, she spotted something shiny the cat had been pawing at. Stooping down to push the weeds apart, she found a long, shiny knife. Holding on to Snowball, she stood up and held the knife up for Joe to see. "Look, Joe, look!"

Joe hurried to her, and taking the knife, he said, "That man had this knife in his belt. It must have fallen out in the scramble."

Mandie had to allow Snowball to get down so she and Joe could cut the rope from the bag. Then they rushed over to the man still lying on the ground. The man surprised them by making a sudden move to rise.

"Stay there!" Joe demanded as he held the knife point toward the man. "Tie his wrists together behind him, Mandie, while I hold the knife."

"Whut fer?" the stranger asked as he opened his

eyes and looked up at Joe.

"We are going to tie your hands up, and you are going to take us to where my father is or I may be tempted to use this knife to prod you on," Joe told the stranger. "Turn over on your stomach and put your hands behind you. Now! Right now!"

The stranger gave him a surly look but obeyed. Mandie quickly wound the heavy rope around the man's wrists and tied it in hard knots. It was long enough that she could bring the rope around his waist and tie it again in the back.

"I dunno whut you a-doin' this fer," the stranger mumbled as he rolled over with the rope as Mandie pulled on it.

Mandie spotted a chain falling out of the man's pocket and decided to pull it out. Giving it a quick yank, she was startled to see Dr. Woodard's gold watch at the end of it. She held it up. "Joe, your father's watch!" she cried.

Joe quickly moved forward, took the watch, and said, "Man, if you've harmed my father, you will pay for it," he said in an angry voice. "This is my father's watch, so don't tell me anymore that you haven't seen him. Now, where is he?"

The man sputtered for an answer as Mandie finished tying the rope. He managed to sit up on the ground and said, "I won that thar watch in a card game." His eyes shifted and he wouldn't look straight at Joe.

"You either tell me where my father is or you are going to walk all the way back to town and to jail," Joe declared. "And you sure won't get out for a long time, maybe never." He swung the watch in front of the man's face. "This is my father's watch."

"All right, all right. I'll show you where I last saw

him," the man replied, scrambling around in the dirt until he was able to stand up. "And, mind you, I can't guarantee he'll still be thar." He made a clucking sound, and his horse came back out of the bushes.

Joe immediately spotted the rifle in the saddle-bag and ran to get it. Pointing it at the man, he said, "I know very well how to use this, so don't try running away."

The man looked at him, halfway smiled, and said, "You wouldn't shoot a man in the back, would you, now?"

"Depends on who he is and what he is doing," Joe said sharply. "Now, get moving."

"You ain't gonna leave my horse here, are you?" the man asked.

"Grab the reins, Mandie, and lead him along with us," Joe told her. "Let's go, mister. Now!"

As she stooped to pick up Snowball, Mandie glanced at the bag of ammunition and the pistol they had left sitting nearby. "Joe, what do we do with that?" she asked, pointing to the bag and gun.

"Can you drag it out of sight under the porch?" Joe asked, holding the rifle pointed at the man, who was listening and watching.

After she carefully put the pistol in the bag with the ammunition, Mandie managed to push the bag into the weeds under the back porch. She snatched up her white cat and ran to grab the reins. The horse seemed to be tame, so she thought she would be able to handle it. "You walk ahead of me and the horse with that gun on the man," she said. "If he tries to run away, I'll run him down with the horse."

"You fergit that's my horse," the man called back to her as they started out of the yard.

"It may be your horse, but I know how to make him run," Mandie yelled back at the man.

"And I know how to shoot your rifle," Joe added. "Now, get going! Which way?"

"Up the mountain," the man replied as he began walking toward the road with Joe following and Mandie and the horse behind. Snowball clutched his mistress's shoulder.

Mandie was anxious to ask questions, but she knew it wouldn't do to divert Joe's attention for a second from the man. She realized Joe and the man must have had some kind of conversation before she joined them. Evidently Joe had told the man he knew he was the one who had come to the Shaws' house for his father. She wondered if the man had denied it. She also wondered what was in the bag the man had tied to the saddlebags.

"Snowball, please be still," she told the cat as he wiggled in her one arm. She bent her head and rubbed his head with her cheek. He settled down and began to purr.

The stranger led them on up the main road until they came to a trail that was barely visible, leading off to the left and going up the mountain. As the man left the main road and stepped onto the trail, Mandie and Joe followed.

"You'd better not be trying to play any tricks," Joe warned the stranger. "Just where does this pathway go?"

"All the way to the top of the mountain. Only we ain't goin' that fur," the man replied, glancing back as he walked on ahead.

Joe looked back at Mandie. The trail was awfully rough and narrow for a horse. "Stop, Mandie," he said, turning sideways so he could keep the gun aimed at the stranger while he spoke to Mandie. "Tie that horse to a tree over there. Someone can come back and get him. You'll have too much trouble getting him through all this."

The man stopped to look back and watch.

"I was wondering how I'd ever manage," Mandie replied as she led the horse off the track. She managed to get the reins tied around a young sapling with Snowball still hanging on to her shoulder. The horse looked at her with sad eyes, and she patted his head and said, "Don't worry, old boy. We'll be back."

As she followed Joe and the man on up the trail, she glanced back at the huge animal. He seemed to be watching her.

After a while the trail became awfully steep. Mandie kept catching on to branches along the way to keep from sliding down in the loose rocks. Snowball clung to the shoulder of the coat and meowed now and then in protest of the rough ride. She was beginning to wonder how much longer the pathway could be when the man suddenly stopped.

"Thar's a cabin over to the left right above hyar," the man said. "And my buddy and the doctor's in thar. But you gonna hafta let me go ahead, 'cause if my friend sees you holdin' that gun on me, he'll start shootin'. That I can guarantee."

"Mister, I'm not that dumb," Joe quickly answered. "I'll decide how we are going to do this when we get there. Just you keep on moving." He held the rifle still pointed at the man.

The stranger shrugged his big shoulders, made an angry face at Joe, and walked on. Joe followed with Mandie behind him.

Mandie wondered exactly how they would

handle this situation. She figured Joe was thinking that if he let the man go on ahead, the man would then circle around out of sight, head back down the mountain, grab his horse, and get away. And there was no guarantee there really was a cabin where the man had indicated.

But what if there really was a cabin up there with another man holding Dr. Woodard at gunpoint? What would they do then? She couldn't discuss it with Joe without the stranger overhearing what they said. This could be a really dangerous matter.

In a few minutes they rounded a bend in the trail, and there was the cabin ahead, just like the stranger had said, on the left-hand side. Suddenly Mandie had an idea that would solve the problem.

"Joe," she said in a loud whisper. "Let's talk a minute."

Joe glanced back quickly and then told the stranger, "Stop right there and don't move another inch."

The man stopped, glanced back at Joe, and then leaned his shoulder against a tree, with his hands still tied behind him.

Joe stepped back, still holding the rifle pointed at the stranger. "He was telling the truth about a cabin being up here," he whispered to Mandie. "But we don't know whether anyone is in it."

"That's what I wanted to talk about," Mandie said, holding Snowball tightly with both hands as he tried to get down. "I have an idea. Suppose I let Snowball down and then I go up and knock on the door of that cabin and ask if they've seen my cat? You could hold the stranger at the back of it, where they couldn't see you from inside, but you could see me. What do you think?"

"Mandie, I don't want to put you in any more danger," Joe said in a low voice.

"But if your father is in danger, we have to try," Mandie protested. "If there is a man inside that cabin holding your father, then Dr. Woodard would see me and would know that you or somebody else is here to help. Then he would be prepared to help us in some way or other."

"But if the man inside is holding my father, he must have a gun. Otherwise, my father could just walk out and go home," Joe told her.

"Another thing that I'm wondering about, Joe," Mandie whispered. "Where is your father's horse and buggy? I don't believe he could have made it up this tiny trail in the buggy."

"I've been thinking about that," Joe spoke softly. "They are bound to be somewhere at the bottom of this trail. Also, if there is another man in the cabin, where is his horse? I don't think anyone would be up in here without some means of transportation."

"Joe, please let me just go up and knock on the door, like I said, and ask if they've seen my cat," Mandie whispered.

"But the man inside would definitely know you wouldn't be up here alone in this isolated place, Mandie," Joe insisted.

"What else are we going to do?" Mandie asked.

"I haven't decided yet. I'm going to get that stranger to move around behind the cabin where I hope there's no windows, and then we can figure out what to do," Joe told her. He started to move back toward the man.

"All right," Mandie reluctantly agreed.

She stood still and watched while Joe motioned

for the stranger to walk on up behind the shack. Then she followed far enough to see what the building looked like. There weren't any windows on either of the two sides they could see.

As soon as Joe had the man positioned in back of the cabin, Mandie called softly, "All right, Joe, here goes Snowball." She quickly let the white cat down, and to her astonishment, Snowball ran directly toward the cabin. He must have smelled food.

Joe looked at Mandie in exasperation as she softly stepped up the hill and reached the door of the cabin. She raised her fist, took a deep breath, and knocked hard.

The door slowly opened and a man with a bandage around his head and another one covering his right arm appeared in the doorway.

"Mister, my cat has run away. I was wondering if you had seen him," Mandie said in a loud voice.

She immediately heard a loud cough from inside the cabin that had to be Dr. Woodard. The man frowned as he looked at her and then turned far enough that she could see a gun in his left hand.

"Haven't seen any cat up here, miss," the man replied. "Where did you come from, anyway? Nobody lives up this way. Who's with you, anyhow?" He leaned out to look over her head. When he did, Snowball came running to the door and pushed his way inside the cabin.

"Oh, there he is," Mandie exclaimed, trying to see inside. "He went off last night and has not been home since. I wonder how he got all the way up here to your house. Could I just come in and get him?"

Mandie noticed the man kept staring at her. She didn't like to be stared at. She reached to straighten her tam and asked, "Why do you keep looking at me like that? Is there something wrong with my hat or something?''

''No, no, miss. You look just fine,'' the man replied. ''It's just that you're the spitting image of someone else I used to know.'' He had a sad voice and a sad look on his face.

''Used to know? You don't know her any longer?'' Mandie asked.

''No, miss, she was my only daughter,'' the man explained. ''Fever took her three years ago in spite of the efforts of Dr. Woodard to save her.''

''Dr. Woodard? You know Dr. Woodard?'' Mandie asked, her heart beating fast.

The man didn't answer but threw the door wide open, placed the gun on a table behind him, and said, ''I give up, Dr. Woodard.'' And as he stepped aside, Mandie saw Dr. Woodard sitting on the other side of the table.

''Oh, Dr. Woodard!'' she cried, running around to embrace him. ''Are you all right? We've been so worried. Joe is outside. Wait, let me go get him.''

''I'm fine, Miss Amanda,'' the old doctor told her with a big grin.

Mandie rushed back outside and yelled, ''Joe, come on. It's all right. Your father is in here.'' She stepped back inside and saw Snowball jump up into the doctor's lap.

Joe came rushing to the doorway, ordering the stranger inside, ahead of him, then he stepped into the cabin. He looked at the second man and then hurried to his father. Mandie's eyes filled with tears as she watched them hug each other. She looked around the room and saw that the first stranger had sat down on a wooden crate. Then she was amazed to see the second stranger on his knees, praying softly.

"Are you all right?" Joe asked his father.

"Yes, son," Dr. Woodard told him. "These two men were holed up, getting ready to rob the bank in Franklin, but Walter Dickens there was injured when his horse ran away with him. So the other man got me to come out here."

"Bank robbers?" Mandie exclaimed. "These men are really bank robbers?"

"No, we ain't no bank robbers," the first stranger spoke up for the first time. "Never got the chance to rob a bank."

Mandie leaned over to whisper to Dr. Woodard, "That man is praying."

"That's right," Dr. Woodard said with a big smile. "I've been working on him ever since I came up here. You see, I knew his family well, and they were all good people." He paused to look at the man and then added, "By the way, he knew your father. He—"

"Mr. Dickens knew my father?" Mandie interrupted. She ran to stoop down by the kneeling man and said, "You knew my father, Jim Shaw?"

"Yes, miss, I knew Jim Shaw pretty well when we were growing up," the man told her as he rose to sit on one of the wooden crates nearby. "But I never had seen his daughter. It's hard to believe that he and I had daughters who looked so much alike." The man's voice broke.

"I am sorry about your daughter, Mr. Dickens," Mandie told him as she stooped down beside him. "You probably know I lost my father," her voice broke, but she continued on. "So maybe we could be friends, me and you."

"Yes, yes, we must be friends," Mr. Dickens said, reaching to pat her hands.

Mandie squeezed his hand, then she straightened up to look around the room. Suddenly she became focused on the table. Sitting there in Aunt Lou's pan was the last of their turkey. She became almost hysterical as she laughed, looked at Joe, and pointed to the pan. "There. Look," she said. "Your father solved the mystery of the missing turkey for us."

"Not exactly," Dr. Woodard told her. "I didn't know where it came from until Joe just now told me it must have been your mother's." He laughed and added, "It was a pretty good turkey."

"I'm glad you had something to eat while they were holding you here," Mandie said and then asked, "What are we going to do about these men?"

Dr. Woodard stood up and said, "I'm going home as soon as I can find my horse and buggy. We'll let the law worry about these men. They never really got around to robbing the bank, so I don't know what charges can be brought."

"But they kidnapped you," Joe protested.

"No, I would say it was a sick call," Dr. Woodard said. "Mr. Dickens there really needed a doctor, and I was glad to help. I don't believe he will ever try anything dishonest again."

Joe quickly reached in his pocket and pulled out the doctor's watch. "Here is your watch. The other man had it." Joe explained how they had met up with the man.

"I don't believe he's from around here," Dr. Woodard said as the man stared at him and listened to the conversation. "I'll leave it up to Mr. Dickens whether he wants to take the man in or let him go, but right now I'm going home." He walked toward the door and said, "Mr. Dickens, if you need any more medical help, I'll be leaving Franklin next Tuesday. In the meantime, I'll be staying at John Shaw's house."

Mandie immediately remembered that no one at home knew where she and Joe were. And she needed to get back home to organize the going-away party for Joe.

And while they might have solved the mystery of the missing turkey, they still had other unsolved mysteries—the green silk scarf they found and lost, the quilt in the attic with the Cherokee symbols on it, and the old diary book they had found.

Yes, she needed to get home and get things moving.

Chapter 11 / Caught!

As they stood in the doorway about to leave, Dr. Woodard tried to find out where the first stranger had hidden his horse and buggy, but the man would not say one word. He just gave the doctor a mean look. But Mr. Dickens immediately intervened.

"Dr. Woodard, your horse is not too far down the mountain on the left-hand side of the trail," Mr. Dickens explained. "It's the place where we have both been leaving our horses. You can't see it from the trail, but when you come over the rise, look for a dead uprooted oak tree, not very large, and go left from there."

"Thank you, Mr. Dickens, I'm sure we'll find it," Dr. Woodard replied.

"And I thank you, Dr. Woodard, for your medical help and for bringing me to my senses," Mr. Dickens told him.

"I just hope it'll give you a better outlook on the future," the doctor replied.

"Good-bye, Mr. Dickens," Mandie said as she stepped outside, holding on to Snowball. "Don't forget we're friends, and I'll be looking for you to come visit sometime."

"And I thank you, Mr. Dickens," Joe said as he joined Mandie.

"See y'all one of these days," Mr. Dickens replied as he closed the door behind them.

Mandie and Joe followed Dr. Woodard down the trail and soon located the doctor's buggy and horse. Fortunately, another wider pathway split off from there, so Dr. Woodard harnessed up the buggy and slowly led the horse down to the main road.

"I certainly am glad we don't have to walk home," Mandie commented as the three of them stepped into the buggy and Dr. Woodard shook the reins.

"Me too," Joe agreed.

"And I'm glad I don't have to walk home. If we hadn't found my horse and buggy, we'd have had to make it on foot," Dr. Woodard reminded them. "Now I want an accounting of everything that has happened since I left the Shaws' house."

Mandie and Joe related the events while Snowball curled up in his mistress's lap and went to sleep. As they passed the Harrisons' and Stones' houses, they spotted some of the children in the yard and waved to them. Then as they came near Miss Metts's house, they told Dr. Woodard about their conversation with the woman.

"She would like to have another dog, and I told her I would give her one of Samantha's puppies," Joe said to his father.

"We'll bring it to her next time we come to Franklin," Dr. Woodard replied.

"But, Dr. Woodard, Joe won't be coming back to Franklin anytime soon," Mandie reminded him.

"That's right. I just can't get used to the idea of you going off to school, my boy," Dr. Woodard said to Joe. "But you know one thing? I'm so proud of you, I'm just a-bustin' at the seams." He grinned as he looked at his son.

"Thanks, Dad," Joe said, returning the grin.

"Well, count me in, too, much as I dislike the idea of Joe going so far off," Mandie added.

"Sure thing," Dr. Woodard said.

When the three got back to the Shaws' house, Mandie's mother and grandmother were in the parlor questioning Sallie and Jonathan for the thirteenth time about where Mandie and Joe had said they were going. So when Mandie and Joe walked in the front door with Dr. Woodard, everyone began talking at one time. Snowball ran off down the long hallway.

"Dr. Woodard, I know you are worn out," Elizabeth told him. "Now you go right on up to your room and get some rest. If you would like, I'll ask Aunt Lou to bring up a little something to eat to tide you over till suppertime."

"Thank you, that would be fine. I appreciate your hospitality," Dr. Woodard said, picking up his medical bag and his coat and hat from the settee where he had left them. "And don't worry, I'll be down in time for supper."

When he left the room, Elizabeth turned to Mandie and Joe. "I suppose both of you are hungry and tired, too," she said. "Why don't y'all just go out to the kitchen and ask Liza, or whoever is in there, to give y'all a snack, since y'all missed the noon meal." She looked at Mandie, who had removed her coat. "Perhaps you should freshen up first."

"I was going to suggest that, Elizabeth," Mrs. Taft said. "The two of them look like they've been through a dirt hole." She smiled at Mandie. "But I'm glad y'all did it, dear. Otherwise, we might have never known what happened to poor old Dr. Woodard."

"We had to do it, but you know, we still have some mysteries we haven't solved," Mandie replied. "Like—"

"Amanda," Elizabeth interrupted her. "Get upstairs and clean up. We'll listen to this story about mysteries later."

"Oh, but we forgot to tell you, Mrs. Shaw," Joe spoke up. "We found your turkey. My father helped eat it."

Elizabeth looked at him in surprise, and Mrs. Taft laughed as Joe explained what had happened.

Then Sallie and Jonathan wanted to get into the conversation, but Elizabeth firmly sent Mandie and Joe out of the room.

Mandie hurriedly washed up and changed clothes in her room and rushed back downstairs. Joe caught up with her on the steps.

"It didn't take you long, did it?" Mandie teased. They went on down the staircase.

"Not when there's food waiting," Joe replied with a smile.

When they came into the front hall, Mandie saw Snowball playing around the coat-tree. He was growling and scratching at something behind it.

"Snowball, what are you doing? Do you smell a mouse or something?" Mandie asked as she stopped to watch the white cat.

"Whatever it is, he's determined to capture it,"

Joe said. "But I don't think he can quite reach it."

At that moment Snowball pulled his paw out from behind the hall tree with something caught in his claws.

"What have you got, Snowball?" Mandie asked, stooping to untangle his foot. Then she exclaimed, "Oh, Joe, look. It's the green silk scarf." She pulled it out and held it up.

"Snowball probably pulled it out of your pocket when you left your coat hanging here, so there's another mystery solved," Joe said with a laugh.

Mandie thought a moment and said, "You're probably right. He either pulled it out of my pocket or it fell out and somehow got behind the hall tree." She smoothed the long piece of silk material.

"Let's go to the kitchen," Joe reminded her.

"All right," Mandie agreed. "I'll put this scarf up high this time so Snowball can't reach it." She hung it on the top hook.

Aunt Lou was waiting for them in the kitchen. "I heard y'all was back and just plain starved to death," she said, going over to open the warmer in the big iron cookstove.

"Aunt Lou, you done heard right," Joe joked with a grin.

"If you'll let us eat in here at your table, we'll tell you all about our adventures today," Mandie told her.

"I think we can arrange that, my chile. Just y'all pull out some chairs over there at de table and I'll bring on de food," the old woman said, taking out pieces of fried chicken from a pan in the warmer and putting them on two plates. She added biscuits and brought the plates to the table.

"Is that all we can have?" Mandie asked, smiling

at her as she looked at the plates.

"It sho'nuff is," Aunt Lou replied. "Y'all gwine eat supper not too long from now. I'll pour y'all a cup of coffee and bring me one, and we'll talk 'bout what y'all done went and did this mawnin'."

When the three of them had settled down at the table, Mandie began. "First of all, we found your turkey." She looked at the woman and smiled.

"You found dat turkey?" Aunt Lou asked.

"Oh, I just realized we forgot to bring the pan back home," Mandie said, looking at Joe.

"Never you mind 'bout dat pan. Where de turkey be?" Aunt Lou asked.

They explained what had happened, and all Aunt Lou could say was, "Well, thank de Lawd, Doctuh Woodard he had sumthin' to eat."

All the time they were talking, Mandie was trying to think of some way to speak to Sallie about the decorations for the party when Joe wasn't around. She hoped that when they went back to the parlor she could make some kind of sign to Jonathan to draw Joe's attention while she talked to Sallie. But when they returned to the parlor, Polly Cornwallis was there, sitting next to Jonathan on one of the settees and asking questions about where Joe and Mandie had been all day. Elizabeth and Mrs. Taft had left the room.

Stopping in the doorway and looking around the room, Mandie asked, "Oh, where is Grandmother? I need to ask her something." She thought that maybe she could get away from Joe this way. Joe went on into the room and sat down.

"She and your mother went for a walk around the yard to get some fresh air," Jonathan told her.

"Sallie, maybe we should go out for some air,"

Mandie said, going on into the parlor.

Everyone laughed. Mandie frowned as she looked at them.

"From what I hear, you've been out in the fresh air all day," Jonathan said.

"Mandie, what did those two men look like?" Polly asked.

"One was a bad-looking man, but the other one, Mr. Dickens, knew my father," Mandie told her. Turning back toward the door, she said, "I think I'll go outside a minute and speak to Grandmother. I'll be right back."

At that moment she heard the front door open, and her mother and Mrs. Taft appeared in the hallway as she looked out. They were taking off their coats and hanging them on the hall tree. Elizabeth went on down the hallway.

Suddenly Mrs. Taft said, "My goodness! There's my scarf. I wondered where it disappeared to." She pulled the green scarf off the hook.

Mandie hurried out into the hallway. "Grandmother, is that your scarf?" she asked.

"Why, yes, Amanda, it is," Mrs. Taft told her as she draped the scarf over her coat on another hook.

"But we found it outside in the yard," Mandie explained.

"In the yard? I don't know how that could be," Mrs. Taft said. "I brought it down here Christmas Day and then decided not to wear it. I left it hanging here on the coat-tree."

"But we did find it in the bushes in the yard the day after Christmas. It was on Thursday," Mandie insisted. She looked back into the parlor and said, "Didn't we?"

The other young people had overheard the conversation, and they all came out into the hall.

"Yes, ma'am, we did find it in the bushes," Sallie confirmed.

"We certainly did," Jonathan agreed.

Mrs. Taft looked at the young people, and when her gaze met Joe's, he said, "Don't count me in. I had already gone home then."

"So had I," Polly volunteered.

"I don't know what to say to that, but I have not worn it outside since I came here," Mrs. Taft insisted. She picked up the scarf and looked at it.

"The only solution I see is that those men stole the scarf when they stole the turkey," Mandie said.

"One man," Joe corrected her. "Remember, the other man was injured, so he wouldn't have been here stealing a turkey and a scarf."

Mrs. Taft was looking closely at the scarf. "Oh, dear, something has damaged it," she said, holding it up for the young people to see. "Those little puckered places in the material weren't there before."

Mandie quickly inspected it, thinking Snowball's claws might have done something to it, but the spots Mrs. Taft indicated were not caused by sharp claws. They looked as though they were melted places in the material. Then she figured it out. "Those look like something hot touched it, the hot turkey pan!" she exclaimed.

Everyone agreed that the man who stole the turkey must have taken the scarf to keep from burning his hands. But then he found it was too thin, threw it away, and stole the dishrag instead.

"That solves another mystery," Joe said, grinning at Mandie. "You're doing real well today."

"Now, if Uncle John and Uncle Ned would come on back, we might be able to find out about the diary book and the quilt," Mandie agreed as the young people went back into the parlor and Mrs. Taft went down the hall.

"I thought you were looking for your grandmother to ask her something," Jonathan reminded Mandie.

"Oh well, I'll ask her later," she replied and tried to motion to Jonathan to take Joe out of the room.

Jonathan understood and nodded. He looked at Joe and asked, "Another game of chess?"

Joe grinned and said, "Why not? I'll learn enough to beat you eventually. Now, if it was checkers, I'd walk all over you."

"No checkers," Jonathan said, rising. Turning to Mandie, he asked, "I suppose it will be all right for us to use your uncle John's chess set again?"

"Of course," Mandie agreed. She motioned toward the set on the table in the corner. "In the meantime, Sallie and Polly and I are going up to my room to do some things."

"Don't hurry back, unless you want to watch. This game may take a while," Jonathan said, grinning. He and Joe went over to sit at the table.

The girls hurried up to Mandie's room, discussed what kind of decorations they would make, and then went to the sewing room to begin. They soon had enough little rosettes, ribbon dolls with lace dresses, and multicolored streamers made to begin decorating. They slipped down the back stairs, carrying their work, and went into the back parlor, closing the door behind them.

"We can pin some of these streamers on the draperies and hang some of the dolls on the chandelier, don't y'all think?" Mandie asked her friends as they surveyed their handiwork on the table.

"Yes, but remember to make something pretty for the table to surround the cake," Sallie reminded her.

"And maybe we should have a ribbon tied across the door. When Joe opens the door to come in here, it will pop," Polly suggested.

"We don't have much time with the party being tomorrow night and Dr. Woodard and Joe leaving Tuesday," Mandie said as the three worked on the decorations.

"We were going to get straw from your uncle's barn and make little animals," Sallie told Mandie.

"I know," Mandie said as she pinned a streamer on a drape. "But our coats are right down there by the parlor door, and Joe would probably see us get them and ask us where we're going."

"Maybe Liza would get the straw for us," Sallie suggested.

"Oh goodness, I clear forgot about Liza. I promised she could help decorate. I'll run and find her and ask her to get the straw," Mandie said.

Mandie found Liza in the kitchen with Aunt Lou sitting at their table.

"Liza, we're beginning to decorate the parlor, and I want to ask you to do us a favor. We need some straw from the barn, and we can't get our coats without Joe seeing us. Would you get it for us?" Mandie asked the girl.

"Sho'nuff, I will," Liza agreed, rising from the table. She looked at Aunt Lou and asked, "All right?"

"Go right ahead, Liza, and help these girls get that parlor fixed up fo' de party," Aunt Lou told her. "Tomorrow you and me, we bake dat chocolate cake."

The girls worked the rest of the afternoon and finally got the room looking like a party room. They stood back and surveyed their work.

"Everything's just perfect!" Mandie exclaimed. "Y'all please help me see that Snowball doesn't get in this room and mess everything up."

"That would be a catastrophe," Polly agreed.

"Sallie, I hope your grandfather and grandmother get back in time," Mandie said. "I'm not sure Uncle John and Mr. Guyer will be here by then, but we'll have the surprise party anyhow."

Liza looked at Mandie and said, "Let's hope dat choc'late cake don't git stolen tomorrow like dat turkey did."

Mandie smiled at her and said, "You know we found that turkey."

"Aunt Lou she done told ev'rybody." Liza nodded in agreement.

The girls returned to the front parlor, and Mandie signaled to Jonathan that the decorations were finished.

"Who's winning?" Mandie asked as she walked over to watch the chess game.

Joe looked up at her, smiled, and said, "I'm not quite sure yet."

Mandie thought again about how much she was going to miss Joe when he went away to college. He had always been around, and now his visits would be few and far between. At least she was proud of organizing the surprise party for him. She knew he would appreciate that.

Chapter 12 / Surprise!

The next morning, which was Monday, Dr. Woodard went out to call on a few of his patients in Franklin. Liza and Aunt Lou gave strict orders that the kitchen was off limits, and they began baking a huge chocolate cake. Mandie and Sallie went to the sewing room with Elizabeth and Mrs. Taft to wrap the presents they were giving Joe. Jonathan and Joe went for a walk.

"You made a fine choice of a present for Joe," Mrs. Taft remarked as she wrapped the shoeshine set. "I'm sure he'll get some use out of this."

"Yes, and this knife will serve lots of purposes," Elizabeth agreed, tying a ribbon around the neat package.

"I'm glad y'all like what I bought," Mandie said as she wrote a note to Joe in the front of the diary book she had bought him.

"I trust my grandfather will return in time to give Joe an arrow from us," Sallie remarked.

Mandie quickly said, "I heard the front door shut downstairs. I'm going to peek down the stairs and see who it is. We don't want Joe catching us up here with all these presents."

"No," Sallie agreed.

"I'll see who it is, Amanda," Elizabeth said, going to the door. "Mother and I are finished with our gifts." She glanced back at the packages on the sewing table as she went out into the hall.

"I'm going down with you," Mrs. Taft told her daughter as she stepped outside the room to join her. "If it's Joe, we'll entertain him to give you girls time to finish."

"Thank you, Grandmother," Mandie replied as she quickly tied a pencil around the diary book and began wrapping it.

As Mrs. Taft started to close the door behind her, Mandie heard someone call, "Anybody home?" and the voice definitely belonged to Uncle John.

"Sallie, it's Uncle John!" Mandie told her friend as she quickly tied a ribbon around the package. "Come on. Let's go downstairs."

The girls got to the bottom of the stairs not far behind Elizabeth and Mrs. Taft. John Shaw and Lindall Guyer were removing their coats in the front hallway.

"Y'all got back sooner than expected," Elizabeth said as John Shaw stepped over to give her a hug.

"Lindall was ready to do business and found exactly what he was looking for," John Shaw replied.

"Just pure luck," Mr. Guyer said with a smile for Elizabeth.

"Go in the parlor and I'll ask Aunt Lou to bring hot coffee to thaw you out," Elizabeth said, starting to turn back down the hallway.

"Wait, Elizabeth," Mrs. Taft said. "I'll attend to

the coffee for you. You go on in the parlor with John and Lindall.'' She hurried back down the hallway.

Mandie and Sallie followed the men and Elizabeth into the parlor, where the adults sat by the fire and the girls dropped onto nearby stools.

"I want to tell y'all real fast before Joe and Jonathan get back that we're having a surprise party for Joe tonight," Mandie told her uncle and Mr. Guyer. And then she realized the men did not know the Woodards were back and that Joe was going away to school. She talked rapidly, filling them in on the details of everything that had happened while they had been gone. "And, Uncle John, we found some kind of old diary book in the attic. Will you look at it and tell us what it is, please?"

John Shaw smiled at her and said, "Of course, Amanda," and turning to his wife, Elizabeth, he added, "I'm sorry, dear, you were here alone with all this happening."

At that moment Mrs. Taft returned to the parlor and took a chair over near the fireplace. "She wasn't alone, John. I was here."

"Yes, ma'am, and I'm thankful for that," John Shaw said, smiling at the lady.

"Now, if Uncle Ned and Morning Star would get back, everything would be going just fine," Mandie remarked. "I'll run upstairs and get the book, Uncle John."

Mandie went up to her room, picked up the book from her bureau, and returned downstairs to the parlor. By that time Joe and Jonathan had come back from their walk and were talking to Mr. Guyer.

"What kind of mine did you buy, Dad?" Jonathan was asking Mr. Guyer.

"It's a rather unusual kind of mine. It's stuff

called mica, but I understand there is a big market for it right now," Mr. Guyer replied.

"Can we go see it?" Jonathan asked.

"No, Jonathan, we don't have time this trip," Lindall Guyer explained, "but we will come back soon, and I'll show it to you then. In the meantime, Mr. Bond will be handling everything for me, with permission of John Shaw, of course."

"Yes, Jason Bond will hire some help and get things moving. It hasn't been mined in a few years," John Shaw agreed.

Mandie had stood beside her uncle during this conversation, and now she held the old book's loose pages out to him.

"What is this, Amanda? Looks like a lot of paper," John Shaw told her as he shuffled the yellowed sheets of paper.

"We found it behind a drawer in an old wardrobe in the attic," Mandie replied. "Mr. Jason thought it might be an account book for the farm here many years ago."

"Well, yes, it could be, but it's so old I can't make out much of anything on these pages," John Shaw told her. Then he looked up and added, "I know exactly who would be able to help you out on this. Uncle Ned. He lived here, you know, when I was a small boy, and he helped my father with the business of the farm."

"All right, we'll ask him," Mandie agreed, taking back the loose papers. "He's supposed to be back anytime now."

But Uncle Ned and Morning Star did not return in the afternoon, and Mandie was so busy seeing about the party for Joe that first thing she knew, it was time for supper.

At the dining table that night, everyone seemed quiet, waiting for the surprise to happen. And everyone knew they would not get any dessert at supper. Everyone, that is, but Joe.

As soon as they were finished, Joe looked at Mandie and said, "I suppose we're going to have chocolate cake for dessert."

Mandie almost choked on the last sip of her coffee, trying to think of an answer, but her mother saved her.

"We'll have coffee and cake later," Elizabeth said, rising from the table. "That way we can get comfortable and have a chance to talk, since Joe and Dr. Woodard are leaving tomorrow for that long journey to New Orleans."

Everyone agreed as they rose and left the room as Mandie had requested earlier. "Son, let's step out on the porch for a whiff of fresh air," Dr. Woodard said, getting his coat from the hall tree.

"Sure, Dad," Joe agreed, reaching for his coat. As he and his father went toward the front door, he called back to Mandie, "I'll be back in a few minutes."

"All right," Mandie agreed.

As soon as Dr. Woodard and Joe went outside, the others all rushed to the back parlor, slipped inside, and closed the door. The huge baby grand piano was in this room, and Mandie immediately approached her grandmother. "You are making me take piano lessons at school because you said every well-educated young lady should know music, but you have never played for me. I don't believe you know how." She grinned.

"Amanda, I am well aware of your tactics. You are only trying to get me to play for Joe's party,"

Mrs. Taft said, smiling down at Mandie. She walked over to the piano and asked, "What would you like?" as she raised the lid on the keyboard.

Mandie frowned and said, "Something fast, or funny, nothing slow and sad."

Mrs. Taft smiled at her and immediately broke into "Hello, ma Baby, hello, ma honey—"

Just as Mandie started to protest, the door opened and Dr. Woodard ushered Joe into the room. Everyone applauded and began congratulating him on his admission to college. The huge chocolate cake stood in the middle of the table in the center of the room, and coffee and cups were nearby. Joe could only stand there and stare.

"Come on, you have to cut the cake," Mandie said, going to grab him by the hand.

At that moment Polly and her mother appeared at the doorway. Elizabeth went to meet them and said, "I'm sorry. We should have waited for y'all."

"No, we're late. Sorry," Mrs. Cornwallis told her.

"I'll help you cut the cake," Polly said, rushing across the room to take Joe's other hand.

Everyone laughed as John Shaw said, "My goodness, Joe, you have so many admirers."

Joe's face turned red, and he immediately pulled away from Mandie and Polly. "I think whoever made this cake ought to cut it," he said, looking around the room.

Aunt Lou, Liza, Jenny, and Abraham were all standing near the doorway, smiling. Joe rushed over to Aunt Lou, caught her hand, and led her to the cake on the table. "I want you to cut it," he said, and then grinning, he added, "but you can give me the very first piece, since you didn't give us any dessert at supper."

"Lawsy mercy," the old woman said, glancing at Elizabeth, who nodded and smiled. " 'Nuff work cookin' dat great big cake. Now I has to cut it, too." She sighed in protest, picked up the knife, and began slicing.

As soon as everyone had their fill of cake, Mandie removed a cover from a corner table and revealed the wrapped gifts. "Now you have to unwrap these," she called out. "We're not going to allow Aunt Lou to do that." She grinned at him.

Joe, who never liked a fuss being made over him, blushed again and finally began to remove the paper and ribbons, thanking each person as the present appeared.

Mandie heard a sudden movement at the doorway to the hallway. She looked across the room and saw Uncle Ned and Morning Star standing there watching. She raced across the room, grabbed both of them by a hand, and pulled them into the room.

"You are late, but there's still plenty of cake and coffee," she told them.

Aunt Lou nodded at Liza, and the girl served them with a slice of cake and a cup of coffee.

Mrs. Taft kept playing the popular music of the day as everyone moved around the room and talked. Then Mandie heard the notes of "When You Were Sweet Sixteen," and she quickly looked at her grandmother. The lady was looking straight across the room at Lindall Guyer, who was staring back.

"Well," Mandie said softly to Joe at her side.

"Yes, there has to have been something between those two many years ago," Jonathan spoke up behind them.

Mandie and Joe turned and agreed.

"Someday I'm going to find out what the story

was," Mandie said. "In the meantime, let's all sit down."

The five young people managed to sit on one settee that was across the room. Mandie asked Joe to tell them about the college.

"But, Mandie, I've told you that I haven't even seen it yet," he said. He turned halfway around to look at her, which put his back to the others, and said, "There's something I've been meaning to say to you. I've thought about it for a long time, and I've decided I should explain so you won't misunderstand what—"

Polly had stood up and was looking at the two as she interrupted, "Oh, Joe, I'm so anxious to see your college. I'm coming down there on a visit— Mother and me. She said so."

Mandie drew a deep breath, stood up, and said, "It's time to show the diary book and the quilt to Uncle Ned. Come on."

All the young people rushed upstairs. Mandie got the book from her room, and then they went on to retrieve the quilt from the attic. Joe volunteered to carry it down the steps. When they reentered the parlor, everyone turned to look.

"What on earth do you have, Joe?" Elizabeth asked.

Before anyone could say anything else, Uncle Ned stepped forward and said, "Cherokee quilt." He reached for it and shook out the folds.

Everyone crowded around with questions.

"My grandfather, what does the story say on the quilt?" Sallie asked.

"Later. Take time to read," the old man told her.

"Will you read it before you leave?" Mandie asked.

Uncle Ned shook his head and said, "Take quilt

home. Get Uncle Wirt read."

"But can't you read it?" Mandie asked.

"Yes, but long time. Wirt know better, faster," the old man said. He folded the quilt and handed it to Morning Star. "Take home."

Mandie was disappointed, but she picked up the pages of the diary book from where she had laid them on a table and handed these to the old man. "Can you tell us what this is?" She explained how they found it.

Uncle Ned scanned the pages and said, "Book for farm. Father of John Shaw make this."

"I figured it was," John Shaw said, standing nearby. "So it was my father's."

"Yes, old book," Uncle Ned agreed.

Mandie looked at her friends and said, "Well, that solves all the mysteries except the quilt. I hope we hear from Uncle Ned on that." She smiled up at the old Cherokee man.

"Fast," he agreed.

It was late that night when everyone went to bed. Mandie couldn't go to sleep. She kept thinking about Joe leaving the next day. The days would be long before she saw him again. She wished she could just go on to the university with Joe, but Joe was two years older and two years ahead of her in school. Then, too, she might not go to the same college. Oh, she was going to miss him more than she would let anyone know. And she secretly believed that Joe would miss her, too. At least she hoped so.

Everyone was up early the next morning, since Dr. Woodard and Joe would be going to the depot. Mandie wished she could have some time alone with Joe, but the house was full of people who wanted to tell Joe good-bye. Then she had a wonderful surprise.

As soon as breakfast was finished, John Shaw rose, looked around the table, and said, "I don't know about you people, but I think I'd rather just tell Joe good-bye right here and not tramp down to that smoky old depot."

Everyone agreed, but everyone also looked at Mandie, who had not said a word. She understood that they were all allowing her to have her own private good-bye with Joe. She felt a rush of love for them all.

So Abraham drove them to the depot in John Shaw's rig. Dr. Woodard sat on the front seat and kept talking to Abraham. Mandie, with Snowball in her lap, and Joe sat in the back, and neither one could think of a single word to say. Joe reached and squeezed her hand as he helped her down at the depot.

"Here she comes!" Dr. Woodard said loudly to Abraham, who was unloading their luggage.

Abraham took the bags inside and checked them. Dr. Woodard walked down the platform. Mandie and Joe stood silently watching the train come in.

"Cheer up, it'll be summertime before we know it," Joe told her. "Maybe Jonathan will come back, and we can go see his father's mica mine. That would be interesting."

"Yes," Mandie replied, dropping her gaze so Joe wouldn't see the tears rapidly filling her blue eyes. Snowball clung to her shoulder, the noise of the train frightening him.

The conductor jumped down from the train and yelled, "All aboard! All aboard!"

Dr. Woodard was down the platform and motioned for Joe to come. Joe looked down at Mandie and said over the noise of the hissing train, "Behave yourself and don't get caught up in any mysteries you can't solve while I'm gone." He quickly planted a kiss on her cheek and raced off down the platform to join his father.

Mandie stood there alone, watching Joe enter the train. As the train started pulling out of the station, he appeared at an open window and yelled back at her, "I forgot to tell you—"

The next few words were indistinguishable above the roar of the train, but she caught the end of it, "I will write to you about this." He leaned out and threw a kiss with his fingers.

Mandie burst into tears as she watched the train disappear down the long tracks. Joe was gone.

Abraham softly came up beside her and asked, "Miss 'Manda, you be wantin' to go back home now?"

Mandie nodded and turned to walk with the old man toward the rig. What had Joe been trying to tell her? She couldn't make any sense out of it as she kept repeating the only words she could understand. He had said he would write, but it would probably take a long time for a letter to get to her from all the way down in New Orleans.

In the meantime, it was going to be a long good-bye.

———

Look for Mandie Book 31, *Mandie and the Buried Stranger*, to be published in June 1999. Mandie and Joe find a stranger buried in a strange way. Who is he? How did he get there?

Great Gifts for MANDIE

The **MANDIE Datebook** is a reminder of birthdays and other important dates. Highlights occasions Mandie holds dear! Hardcover, $10.99.

The **MANDIE Diary** is a perfect place to write special thoughts. Features a brass lock and key! Hardcover, $12.99.

SNOWBALL Stationery is the purr-fect way to write letters to friends—or fan letters to author Lois Gladys Leppard! Timesaving tri-fold stationery includes self-adhesive stickers to seal notes-no envelopes needed. Set of 12 notes and stickers, $8.99.

fans!

SNOWBALL,
Mandie's constant
companion and
loyal friend, can
now be yours! This
adorable 5" tall,
plush bean bag toy has soft "long-
hair" fur, blue gem eyes, and a name tag collar. $10.99.

MANDIE'S *Cookbook* is
filled with Mandie's favorite
recipes as well
as the fascinating
experiences of girls from
the turn of the century.
Spiral Binding, $12.99.

**Available now at your favorite bookstore,
or send check or money order to:** Bethany House Publishers
Attention Customer Service
11400 Hampshire Avenue South
Minneapolis, Minnesota 55438

BETHANY HOUSE PUBLISHERS